Acknowledgements

I would like to thank my husband Sean for being so supportive throughout this process.

For listening to all of my crazy ideas and plot twists and for always letting me know he believes in me.

I couldn't have done this without you Dute,

Thank you x

Dedications

I would like to dedicate this book to my children.

Alex, Sophie, Rebecca and Melissa

You are my world x

1

I lay restlessly under the covers. I watched the seconds on the clock tick by, waiting for the moment to arrive. The room was still in darkness, shadowy shapes played with my imagination.

By the time the sun started to creep through the gap in the curtains, I was filled with anxious anticipation. I watched Ben, his chest gently rising and falling in a steady, deliberate rhythm. The hazy light illuminated his face, kissing his soft, red lips. As I gazed at his form, I felt the need for his touch.

It felt as though I had awaited the day ahead for years. I wondered how Ben could sleep, why he didn't share my overwhelming excitement? I moved in bed hoping to wake him, but he didn't move beside me. I turned from my back to my stomach, bouncing a little as I did, but still no movement. My hand ventured onto his side of the bed as I reached out to touch his toned torso. His body was warm and firm beneath my fingers and touching him sent shivers of delight through my body. I wanted to kiss him, to softly brush my lips against his and feel the warm safety of his embrace. His eyes remained closed, shutting out the world. My lips found his toned shoulder, as I tasted his warm skin excitement rippled down my spine. My heart began to beat a little faster as I longed for his touch. As he started to rouse, I raised an eyebrow "awake are we then Mr?".

"Hmm," he replied in a sexy, sleepy tone. "Didn't have much choice with you rummaging around like a ferret!"

"Aren't you excited?" I could not keep the glee from my voice.

He smiled a wide, warm, loving smile that lit up his entire face. "Yes, I'm excited." He wrapped his arms around my naked back and started to pull me towards him. He gazed toward the alarm clock on the bedside table "But it's six o'clock and we don't need to be there for another four hours! There's no rush." He pulled me closer and kissed my lips. "Plenty of time before we have to leave." He spoke between kisses.

With every touch of his lips against mine, excitement grew in my body. His body pressed against mine I could feel his arousal growing too.

"Hmmm," I replied, "and is there anything you would like to do to pass the time?" I smiled suggestively at him, gazing into his eyes.

His strong hands grasped my hips and he pulled me onto him, raining kisses onto my face and neck as he did. The feeling of his hot, hard erection against my thigh excited me. I felt my nipples harden as he pressed himself against me. I closed my eyes and as I imagined him inside me. I yearned for the feeling of his body penetrating mine. His lips found mine once more. I closed my eyes and lost myself in the deep kiss. As his hands found my full breasts, our bodies started to move together. I wrapped my hands around his neck. I was lost in the moment. My mind empty, the whole world melted away. All that was left was Ben and me. Rhythmically we moved together until we both reached a shuddering climax. As pleasure rippled through my body, I felt overwhelmed by the feeling of love that followed. Ben rolled me onto my back. We lay together, kissing and caressing, enjoying the moment of closeness that we had shared. I was lost in peace and serenity. My thoughts mute as I lay in his arms.

As I awoke once more, I realised I had drifted back to sleep in Ben's arms. I was alone in the bed. I could hear the pitter-patter of the shower inviting me to join Ben. I imagined the delicious sensation of his soapy hands washing my body. My heart skipped a beat as I glanced at the clock. Two hours to get to the hospital. A different form of excitement took hold. I placed my hand on my abdomen. "We're going to see you soon," I whispered.

Ben walked into the bedroom, beads of water clinging to his shoulders, a towel wrapped loosely around his waist. His chest was firm and toned. To me he looked perfect. The way every man should be.

He caught me watching his semi-naked frame. “Hey pervy.” his full lips formed a crooked smirk.

“Don’t you want me to look?” I asked flirtatiously.

“Oh, like you can help yourself.” He wiggled a little, allowing the towel to ‘accidentally’ drop to the floor. “Ooops!”

“I could take it or leave it.” I turned and ambled away, smiling to myself as I left him stood naked and untouched.

A smile played at my lips, how I wanted my lips to touch his.

“Fancy a coffee?” Ben asked as I stepped out of the shower room, towelling my hair.

“Oh, yes please,” I smiled, “But make sure you use the decaf stuff. I’ve read that caffeine can be dangerous.”

“Sure you have,” Ben replied. “You’ll be telling me breathing is dangerous next.”

“We can’t be too careful,” I warned. “I’m almost forty. Having a baby at my age carries a lot of risk. We need to do everything we can to make sure we look after our little one.”

“I know.” He wrapped his arms around me from behind. He gently kissed my shoulder. “But we’re at the twelve-week stage now. The danger has all but passed.”

I nodded and smiled. I felt reassured by his words.

I sat at the breakfast bar sipping at my coffee. My mind was racing with thoughts of the impending scan. My phone beeped to notify me of a message. I glanced at the screen.

Hayley: Good luck for today x

9:30

As I replied "thanks" I tried not to be cross about the hypocrisy of her message. For months she had been warning me of the dangers of pregnancy so close to forty. She had me all but convinced that the baby would be born with disabilities or learning difficulties, that the rest of my life would be spent caring for a child that would never be able to care for themselves.

"You OK?" Ben asked, reading my expression.

"Hayley wishing me luck," I replied.

He nodded, I didn't need to elaborate. He was aware of my increasingly strained relationship with Hayley.

He nodded again. "Don't let her get you down." He tilted his head to the side thoughtfully then smiled as an idea formed in his mind. "Hey, maybe it'd be nice to get away for a few days," he took hold of my hand, "before you start to show properly."

"Sounds nice, where to?" I asked.

"I'd like to go back to Barcelona," he replied. I smiled at the thought.

"It would be a little tamer than the first time we went," I pursed my lips playfully as I was transported back to the beautiful city in my mind.

I could almost feel the sun penetrating my skin as Ben and I lay on the grass in Park Guell. Our stolen kisses raising the eyebrows of passing tourists.

"It'd be our last trip with just the two of us," Ben winked.

"Apart from our little stowaway," I smiled again.

I was filled with happiness. My life was as close to perfect as I could ever have wished. I fought against the wave of sadness as my thoughts drifted to my former life. I was determined to remain positive. What had gone before was in the past. My future with Ben was now and I loved every moment of our lives together.

The journey seemed to take forever. I clutched my appointment letter, my eye nervously on the clock. My bladder full. Every movement of the car added to the pressure, making me feel as though I could barely hold on.

"Are you ok?" Ben stroked my knee reassuringly.

"I'm fine," I smiled back at him. "I really need to go to the loo though!"

He laughed a little, "I told you that three glasses of water was way too much."

"It says to have a full bladder."

"Not that full!" I could see a smile playing at his lips.

"How about Freddy?" Ben tried to distract me with the game we had played for the last eight weeks, ever since I got a pink line on the test.

I enjoyed the game. Enjoyed the fantasy of our child. The idea of holding our baby in my arms, of feeding, nurturing, teaching and guiding our child. I had imagined our baby a thousand times. I could see the bright and inquisitive green eyes, full red lips and a cheeky smile. Blonde hair with a whisper of a curl. Our child was beautiful, funny, intelligent and I loved him or her. I had loved our baby the moment I saw the positive test. Over the past eight weeks that love had grown. I would hold my stomach and think of him or her nestled securely inside me. I would try to telepathically communicate to the developing child. I spent far more time than I should looking at images of the various stages of development, what to expect at four weeks, five weeks and beyond. I marvelled at the rapid development from almost nothing to a tiny human being in the matter of a few weeks.

"Mmm, not sure," I replied. "I quite like old fashioned names, but that makes me think of Queen."

He laughed, "Ok, Brian?"

"Still Queen!"

He laughed again. I looked at him and smiled, a rush of love came over me. I felt so lucky that we were at the start of this amazing adventure together, my best friend and my lover. Today we would see our baby for the first time. I could barely wait.

"Henry?" I offered. "We seem to do a lot of boys names, do you think it will be a boy?"

"I think it will be a girl, to be honest." He paused thoughtfully, "It would be nice to have a daughter."

"I'll just be happy to have a healthy baby." I knew that was a lie. I wanted a girl too deep down, but I didn't want to feel disappointed if it turned out to be a boy.

"So long as it's not ugly," he added. I snorted and almost lost control of my full bladder in shock.

"You can't say that!"

"Who says?"

"I do!" I mocked shock. "We will love it regardless!"

"You might." He grinned and winked at me.

"You will!" I insisted. "Besides, all children are beautiful to their parents."

"Hmm, not so sure about that." He replied.

I glanced over at Ben and smiled inwardly. I knew that no child of his could ever be plain let alone ugly. Our baby was destined to be beautiful. I hoped it would share his soft fair curls and full red lips. I longed for our baby to have his expression filled green eyes, I longed to look into a second pair of those eyes and see the love I saw when I looked at Ben.

I wondered how different I would have been if my past had been different. Would Ben and I still share this bond if our lives had been different? I tried to tell myself that everything happened for a reason and that Ben had been sent to me when I needed him most. In my darkest of days when my soul had been sad and lonely and devoid of love, Ben had come into my life and made me complete. He had given me a reason to live and a reason to love. He set my soul on fire with love and passion, he excited me more than I had imagined possible.

2

The hospital waiting room was small and dark. Red plastic chairs lined the walls. A clock on the wall ticked off the seconds as I waited. Nervously I looked at Ben. He reached for my hand, took it in his and squeezed gently.

“Did anyone ask why we had both booked off the same day?” Ben asked.

“That new girl Millie who they’ve sent to work with me was asking what we were doing. I said we wanted to do some shopping. I told her it’s my fortieth in a few weeks and that we might have a party so I wanted to look for a new outfit.”

“Do you want a party?” He asked.

“I don’t know,” I replied honestly. “The idea of a party is probably way better than an actual party.”

He laughed, “Why’s that?”

“I don’t really have any friends.” I shrugged. “Who would I invite. It’d be a really shit party with just us two.”

“You have Hayley.” He told me.

“You hate Hayley.”

“I’ll admit I’m not her biggest fan, but hate is a bit strong.”

“So we have you, me and Hayley so far.” I laughed a little, “Sounds like a great party.”

"There's David too." Ben couldn't avoid smirking as he spoke. "And Josh the prodigal son."

"The perfect line up," I spoke sarcastically.

We sat in silence for a moment. I glanced around the room.

"Maybe that weekend away would be a better idea." I thought of our earlier conversation. "Just you and me."

"Maybe," Ben replied, squeezing my hand a little. "But wouldn't that feel like letting it go by unmarked?"

"What makes you think I want to mark it?" The jokey nature was gone from my voice. "I'm not over the moon about turning forty." I hushed my voice as I glanced around the room. "Just look around you, how many other pregnant forty-year-olds can you see?"

"You don't look forty." He replied. "You should be proud of the shape you're in."

"Don't get me wrong Ben," I looked him in the eye. "I'm glad that we're having this baby. Wow! That is such an understatement. I am completely in love with this baby. I can't wait to see him or her. To hold it in my arms, to protect it from everything."

He slipped his hand onto my abdomen in a symbol of solidarity. His way of showing that he felt it too.

"I'm not glad to be turning forty." I sighed as I spoke. "I wish we had done this ten years ago when I wasn't facing the thought of being the oldest mum on the delivery ward."

"Lots of women are having babies later in life now."

"Yes." I agreed. "That's true, but that doesn't stop me from wishing we had done it sooner."

~

I cast my mind back to ten years earlier when my thirtieth birthday had been looming like a dark cloud.

Ben had been working at Eco Build for a couple of years. I wasn't sure how we had become friends. It started so slowly at first, but it developed naturally. He would call by my desk at lunchtime with a sandwich and coffee giving an order not to skip lunch again. He sent me stupid jokes in the middle of the night and I would be woken by a notification on my phone telling me that I had a text from Ben. Excitedly I would open the message, only to be disappointed that it was yet another awful joke. Soon we were best friends. We spent more time together than many of the couples we knew, but I never seemed to tire of his company.

It was early one Monday morning when Ben called at my desk.

"It's your birthday next week," he announced.

"Is it?" I asked sarcastically.

"So, what are you doing to celebrate?" he asked.

"I'm going to treat myself to an extra hour in the office," I smirked. Ben was always pulling my leg about working too many hours.

"Is that so?" He asked playfully. "If those plans are set in stone then I understand."

"I think they are," I replied.

"I have a better idea." He said.

"Oh yes?" I looked up from my drawing board. "Let me guess, you're playing five a side again and you need someone to stand in the freezing cold cheering you on?"

"Not this time." He laughed.

"Your parents are coming for dinner and you need someone to cook for you and pretend to be your girlfriend?"

"They'd never fall for that one after last time when you messed the whole thing up."

"I swear it was like that Gerard Depardieu film where they have to pretend to be married so he could stay in America." I laughed at the memory.

"They liked you though." He smiled broadly. "Dad is always asking what happened to that pretty girl Hope."

"Don't lie." I laughed. "Your mum was horrified. Especially when she discovered the take-out containers in the bin." I giggled at the memory of me trying to pass off the Thai dishes as my own and Ben's Mum continually commenting that the food was every bit as good as that Thai takeaway down the road.

"What I have planned is much more fun." He tried his best to assure me.

"Another twenty-mile bike ride?" I asked.

"Nope," he laughed. "and don't try to make out that you didn't love that."

"I loved all of the pit-stops in the pubs along the way." I winked with a wry grin. "Admittedly though, you do know all of the best pubs with beer gardens."

"I really do." He nodded. "We should do that again. It was such a fun day, although I swear that copper was ready for doing us for being drunk in charge of a bicycle."

"Yeah," I agreed, "good job he got that emergency call."

"Yes," he laughed exaggeratedly, "then you wanted to go after him on the bikes because you wanted to know what the call was."

"I'm concerned about public interest issues." I protested.

"You're bloody nosey." He said. I pouted.

"So, what's your big idea this time?" I asked to change the subject.

"Karaoke." He announced, clearly very proud of himself.

I frowned. "Isn't that a bit 1994?"

"It's retro." He told me.

"Retro?" I rolled my eyes. "You're so funny."

"I'm hilarious, that's what you love about me." He gave me one of his most charming looks.

"That's Blue Steel right there," I smirked.

"So, we're going to Karaoke for your birthday."

"No." I groaned. "I can't sing and neither can you, I have no intention of watching a load of X Factor wannabes trying to get noticed."

"It'll be fun." He argued. "There's this great little bar in Manchester that Steve told me about. Check this, it's a Japanese tempura bar but they do Karaoke on Friday nights."

"Oh please." I protested. "Not another one of Steve's recommendations!"

"I've booked a table for us at eight-thirty on Friday." He grinned. "I'll pick you up at twenty past seven. I'll leave the car at the station and we'll jump on the train."

"But then we'll miss the last train home like we always do and it'll cost us a fortune for a taxi." I protested.

"We'll make sure we don't miss the train." He promised. "Hope it'll be fun, I swear."

Ben arrived at my flat at seven o'clock. In his hands was a huge bouquet and a bottle of wine.

"Happy Birthday." He greeted me, kissing me lightly on the cheek. I savoured the feeling of his skin against mine.

"Thank you." I took the flowers from him. "You shouldn't have."

He really shouldn't have. I hated flowers. I always viewed them as an unwanted responsibility. I would have to find a vase, cut the stems, arrange them in a way that looked pretty and then I would have to make sure I changed the water in a couple of days. Who needs a burden like that?

"You look stunning." I could feel Ben's eyes on my body, drinking in every curve and dip. "If you pull tonight then don't bring him back to our room."

"Our room?" I questioned.

"Yeah, I hope you don't mind but I've booked a hotel in Manchester. Nothing too fancy, but I thought about what you said about the train and the taxi." He saw the shocked expression on my face. "There's nothing untoward about it. I booked a twin room, I just figured we could stay out and have a laugh."

"Oh," I tried to gather my thoughts. I felt nervous yet excited at the same time. "you didn't say. I haven't packed."

"Go and put some PJ's and some jeans in a bag, you don't need anything else."

I laughed to myself as I headed for my bedroom. Ben didn't know much about women! I considered myself pretty low maintenance, but I certainly needed quite a lot more in my overnight bag than a pair of jeans and my PJ's. As I packed I felt a stab of disappointment. I had hoped that one day I would need an overnight bag for a night with Ben, but I had also hoped that it wouldn't include pyjamas.

For once Steve's recommendation was spot on. The food was delicious and we washed it down with a ridiculous amount of sake. I didn't notice when the karaoke started. When I became aware of out of key voices I turned towards the glittery stage in the rear of the bar.

"Oh my god!" I rolled my eyes. "Listen to them, my bloody cat sounds better."

"Yeah," Ben agreed. "Even we could do better than those two."

"Absolutely." I held my hand up for a high five, he didn't disappoint.

"So, what are we singing?" He asked.

I laughed. "I'm not that drunk." Ben beckoned to the waiter.

"Could we have more sake please?"

As the song came to an end the room erupted into a mix of applause and laughter. The two guys singing took a gracious bow. I was impressed with their ability to laugh at themselves.

The host arrived on stage wearing an awful purple shimmering suit.

"Thank you to Henry and Barry there singing 'My Heart Will Go on.' well-done lads." There was another gentle ripple of applause. "Next up we have an unusual karaoke request, but I'm a bit of Radiohead fan so I'd like to see how they carry this one-off." I cringed. I loved Radiohead. The idea of having a song by one of my favourite bands obliterated by a tone-deaf idiot was painful.

"Singing Creep by Radiohead we have Ben and Hope." I looked at Ben in absolute horror. He was gurning stupidly.

"Tell me that's not us." I glared at him as I spoke.

"Come on." He told me as he grabbed for my hand.

"I don't believe you." I pulled my hand away.

"It's your favourite song." He told me. "It'll be fun, come on."

"Come on down guys." Coaxed the host.

Reluctantly I followed Ben to the stage.

I felt nervous standing on the stage, I looked around and realised that the majority of people were eating and drinking, barely paying attention to us.

The opening bars to Creep started. The guitar playing the tune I had listened to a thousand times. Drums keeping the beat.

In front of us, a TV monitor displayed the lyrics for the first few lines. I felt the music take control of me, shivers went through my spine as I listened to the track that spoke to me. The track that defined me, the track that felt more personal than any other. I allowed the room to melt away. Suddenly there was nobody else in the room. Just Ben and I, microphones in hand.

Ben looked at me as he sang the opening lines, he smiled, encouraging me to join in. I looked at Ben. I sang to him. I wanted him to understand how I felt about him. I wanted him to understand what held me back. Why I had barriers around me. I needed to protect myself from being hurt. His eyes penetrated mine, he seemed to be searching my soul. I looked back at him, my eyes brimming with unspent tears, my lips burning with the desire to brush them against his.

As the song came to a finish the room was again filled with applause.

"Thank you so much, Ben and Hope." The host spoke into his microphone. "Now go get a room the pair of you!"

I blushed.

Out on the street, we were still laughing at our terrible karaoke debut.

"Well, I can knock that one off my bucket list," I told Ben laughing. "I can't believe you made me do that."

"I didn't make you." He protested.

"You bloody did." I pushed his arm playfully. "You bugger."

"It was fun."

"We were soooo bad," I said kicking off my shoes. "I'm going to have to go barefoot, these shoes are killing me."

"I'll give you a piggyback." He crouched and held his arms ready to grip onto me. "Jump on."

"You'll drop me!" I objected.

"No chance, jump on."

"You'll regret this," I told him as I hitched up my skirt and jumped onto his back.

He lifted me from the ground in one swift move, his strong arms holding my legs. I rested my head against his back. My arms gripping his firm torso. The scent of his aftershave mingled with pheromones filled my nostrils and sent me dizzy with desire. I closed my eyes as we made our way haphazardly down the street.

"Hey there!" He jiggled slightly. "You better not be going to sleep."

"Just enjoying the ride," I whispered.

"Mmmm." He stopped. He lowered me to my feet then took my hand and coaxed me towards a nearby bus shelter.

He faced me. My back against the glass of the shelter, his body close to mine.

"You amaze me, Hope." I looked at him in confusion. "Every day you face the world with that steely determinism. Every day you work so hard to make a difference."

I laughed in a bid to brush off his complement.

"You should never feel like a creep." He started to sing again, hideously out of tune. "You float like a feather, in a beautiful world." He kissed me softly on the lips. My spine tingled, I was under his spell. "You're so very special." He kissed me again, deeper this time, his body pressing against mine. I responded hungrily. My hand wrapping around his body. He pressed himself against me. I could feel his erection pressing against me.

I felt panic rising inside me. I felt confused, hurt and angry. This was Ben. This was my best friend. This was the guy who ordered pizza to arrive at the office when he drove past my flat and realised I wasn't home yet. This was the guy who had brought me cold remedies when I had been ill. He wasn't the guy who took me out, got me drunk and then tried to get me to bed.

I pushed him away firmly. He stood in front of me looking at me in confusion.

"Are you OK Hope?" He asked. "I'm sorry, I thought you wanted me to..."

"We're friends," I told him, tears starting to form. "I thought you thought more of me than trying to add me to your list of hookups."

"No, you've got me wrong." He insisted. "You know what I think of you, or at least you should."

"I know when I'm being played Ben," I shouted as I turned my back and headed over the road. I held out my hand.

"Taxi!" I called urgently.

~

"Hope O'Donnel" called the receptionist.

I grabbed onto Ben's hand and excitedly made my way to the scan room.

The room was small and dark. There was a hospital bed covered in blue hygiene paper in the middle of the room. The scan equipment was in a trolley next to the bed. The radiologist sat on a chair next to the bed. She smiled as we entered the room.

"Hope O'Donnel?" she inquired. I nodded.

"Date of birth?"

"25th May 1978" Did I imagine the raised eyebrows?

"address?"

"72 St George road."

She glanced at my note "first pregnancy?"

"Yes, we're so excited." Ben squeezed my hand. "We've been trying for four years."

"Aw," she smiled a reassuring smile. "If you pop on the bed we'll have a look.

I climbed up onto the bed and laid flat. The pressure from my bladder was becoming painful.

"Just unfasten your jeans a little." She spoke softly. I felt the shock of cold as she squeezed gel onto my exposed abdomen. I tried to watch the screen, desperate to see my little cargo. I could see that she was measuring something, a white blob in the middle of the screen. I waited for her to turn the screen to face us so I could see my little baby.

I glanced from the screen to her face. I read something in her expression that sent a cold shiver down my spine. I could feel the blood draining from my face. I was no longer excited. I was afraid. Something was wrong. I felt sick. My heart was pounding in my chest, my head was spinning. In that moment time stood still. For an eternity the radiologist stared at the screen and took measurement after measurement. Eventually, she turned to me, a well-practised sympathetic look plastered on her face.

I looked at Ben, I asked myself if he had seen it too.

"I'm afraid to tell you that I can't find a heartbeat." The words rang in my ears and I started to feel dizzy. Tears stung my eyes, I fought to hold them back. To cry would be to admit, to accept. I wasn't ready to do either.

The radiologist went on to talk about missed miscarriage, told me that I could give it a week then go back to discuss treatment options. Her words washed over me, barely registering in my comprehension.

In a daze, I stood up. I left the scan room and headed straight for the ladies. In my grief-stricken state, my bladder was still calling.

When I stepped back into the waiting room Ben was stood waiting for me. His green eyes, normally dancing with happiness were brimming with tears, his face a picture of complete sadness and disappointment. In that moment I felt so guilty. I felt selfish and greedy for wanting it all.

I threw my arms around him and buried my face in his shoulder. I fought to hold back the tears. "I'm sorry." I whispered, "I'm so sorry." I repeated the words again and again, barely a whisper from my lips but the words raced through my mind. 'I'm sorry.'

He took hold of my shoulders and held me, forced me to meet his gaze. "There is no need to be sorry." He spoke the words kindly, but firmly, with true conviction. "This is not your fault." When I didn't react he said again more firmly. "this is not your fault and I don't want you to say sorry again." I nodded, but deep down I couldn't shake off the guilt I felt.

In stunned silence I wandered down the hospital corridor. My feet felt too heavy to lift so instead I shuffled, head down, shoulders slumped.

A few hours ago we had it all. But now I felt lost, afraid and desperately empty.

3

We returned home to a desperately quiet house. I sat at the dining room table in silence. My phone flashed with a message from Hayley, "How did it go?" seemed like such a thoughtless question. Hayley meant well. Yet sometimes she would turn situations around and make them about her. Now she was waiting for fantastic news, I could imagine her forced sympathy sprinkled with 'I told you so'. I couldn't face that call.

It all felt so pointlessly and hideously cruel. The baby that we had been in love with for all this time left us shortly after it began to exist. I felt foolish for the times I had gazed at my reflection and saw the baby bump that was starting to develop. There hadn't been a baby, not as such. The being that I had been attached to and loved so much barely had a heart, let alone a brain. I wondered if it had felt pain. I wondered what I had done wrong, what I could have done differently. I wanted to turn back the clock six weeks, when the life inside me was a life. I wanted to make it feel my love so it would stay.

"Do you want a coffee?" Ben's words barely seeped into my consciousness. I was so wrapped up and focussed on my pain and suffering. I glanced up through tear-filled eyes and shrugged. Ben had made three mugs of coffee since we returned from the hospital. I was shutting Ben out, but I couldn't help it. I was consumed with my own pain, I hadn't given much thought to Ben, how he felt and what he wanted. I just wanted to shut out the world, everything. I wanted to isolate myself, protect myself from the pain I was feeling. His hand brushed my shoulder in a soft sign of affection. I felt my shoulders stiffen; my mind screamed 'leave me alone'. I wanted to get lost in my pain and misery. I wanted to fall into the dark pit of despair before me and stay within its dark comforting walls. I had no right to feel love or affection or happiness while my baby remained dead and unborn inside me.

"A week" I muttered, Ben came back through from the kitchen where he had been busying himself when I spoke. I had barely uttered a word since we had left the hospital.

"What was that?" the forced cheerfulness in his voice grated on my nerves.

"A week," I spoke louder this time, almost angrily. "I have to wait a week."

"We both do." he sat down at the table and took hold of my hands. I was tempted to pull my hands away, but I sat passively facing him. "this is happening to both of us." I knew he was right. I knew that he was as much in love with our baby as I was, but a part of my mind screamed out 'Fuck you! This is my body, I'm the one who has to go back and have the baby I want and love ripped out of me.' I didn't scream the words, or utter a sound. I nodded quietly, tears brimming in my eyes.

The next day I was awoken by the sound of Ben shuffling around the bedroom. I opened my eyes a fraction, desperate to keep the world out. Ben was dressed in a work shirt and trousers. His hair styled in his usual perfectly tousled way. He was ready to go. We hadn't discussed work. I had assumed that he would stay home. I couldn't imagine how he could think of anything other than our lost child.

"Do you want me to speak to Derek?" Ben asked. "Let him know you won't be in today?"

"Up to you," I answered indifferently.

"Maybe you'll feel up to it tomorrow?" I was repulsed by his callous nature. His complete disregard for our child.

"Let's at least wait until I'm no longer carrying a dead baby around with me everywhere hey?" My words were sharp and cold and filled with putrid sentiment. The rancid words reminded me of her, of Helen. I shuddered.

"Hope!" Ben was shocked by my words, by my tone. The layers of polite control had been peeled away and I lay before him with my bleeding soul.

I retreated from his gaze. Pulled the duvet up over my head and snuggled down, hiding in the darkness.

"I know you're in shock," Ben spoke matter-of-factly.

"I know we were both expecting good news yesterday, but just because you're not pregnant now doesn't mean you won't be, we can try again." His words angered me even more.

"Just go," I shouted, pulling myself up from my makeshift nest. "Talk to Derek, tell him whatever you like. No! Tell him that I quit. Tell him that there is so much more to life than designing fucking buildings."

"I'll tell him you're ill." He spoke softly. His hand brushed my head fleetingly and then he was gone.

4

My mind wandered as I lay in bed. Drifting between sleep and consciousness. Barely able to process my thoughts.

As sleep took over my wretched body, wild dreams began to fill my mind. Images of tiny bare feet pounding through coarse grass. A cool sea breeze drifting through the warm air and tickling my skin. Butterflies wings fluttering wildly. I felt my body flying through the air, lifted high on the currents. The salty air wrapping me in its chilly embrace. Then I was falling, down and down through the darkness, like Alice down the rabbit hole. Butterflies flitted through the darkness, their wings filled with an eerie luminance. In a panic, I reached out to slow my descent. Grasping in the darkness for something to stop me. I felt the tiny body in my hand. I didn't dare to open my fist and view the contents. I knew what I would find. I landed with a thud. My hands brushed against a rough, short piled carpet. I could sense rather than see the shelves all around. Packs of exercise books, pens and pencils neatly lined up and colour coded. The darkness was stifling. The wings of tiny butterflies shone through the darkness, each one a tiny reminder of a deed, a thought a mistake that I had made. Each one taunting me and filled with accusation. Fear gripped my body as I felt tiny wings brushing against my cheek. I pursed my lips tightly and screwed my eyes shut, terrified that the butterflies would find their way inside my mouth. As soft wings brushed against me, fear had me in its grip. I opened my eyes in search of an exit, I needed to escape.

A crack of light was seeping in through a gap under the door. I lifted myself to my feet, grasping for the handle for the cupboard door. As I twisted the handle, I could feel resistance and an array of giggles erupted from the other side.

"You're such a freak Hope." I could hear Amy's voice. Always Amy.

"Let me out!" I begged. Hot tears rolling down my cheeks.

"Why should I do anything for you?" Her voice dripped with hate. "You and your filthy mother in that beautiful cottage. You don't deserve any of it."

"Let me out." I cried louder. Images of Helen filled my mind. I was suffocated by the emotions that her memory evoked. "I'm not her! I'm not like her."

I looked down. Red liquid oozed into the cupboard. Slowly at first. I stepped back from the door as it crept towards my bare feet. The acrid irony smell filled my nostrils as the liquid flowed faster and faster. Covering my body.

I awoke in a panic. Wrapped in a duvet that seemed to stick to every inch of my body. As I fought with the cover I saw the deep red blood that covered my lower half. I sobbed loudly but there was nobody to hear me, nobody to comfort me.

"I'm so very sorry," I spoke to my child. "I'm sorry I left it so late to make you. I was afraid. I didn't think your Daddy loved me. I didn't think anyone could love me."

By the time I heard Ben's key rattling in the front door I felt completely drained.

I had changed the bedding and showered, then took a bottle wine from the fridge. I had considered drinking straight from the bottle, but as I raised the bottle to my lips, an image of Helen popped into my mind. I reached for a glass instead.

I sat silently at the kitchen table sipping the liquid and waiting for it to push away the thoughts that plagued my mind. The amount of blood I had lost had shocked me. My lips and cheeks felt numb, my body felt weak. I knew that I should seek help, but I didn't care. Bleeding to death seemed quite apt.

"Hope?" Ben spoke softly at first. He peered at me from the doorway. I had barely noticed the darkness that had fallen around me, consumed by my thoughts it didn't matter. I could barely see the puzzled expression on his face, but I knew it was there. "What are you doing?" He laughed in that way he did that expressed his disapproval. Anger rose within me as his chuckle grated on my nerves.

"Having a miscarriage." The words spewed from my lips before I could hold them in. The tone in my voice was cruel and alien to me.

"You're pissed!"

"Tomorrow I'll be sober, but you'll still be a self-righteous prick!" Once more my tone was hurtful. The words I spoke came from the most shattered embers of my mind.

"This isn't my fault Hope." He sounded like a wounded animal.

"No, it's my fault." Tears welled in my eyes. I desperately tried to hold my steely resolve. "It's my fault we left it so late, my fault because I couldn't get my shit together and now our baby has paid the price." I stood up, picked up the glass and swigged back the contents with one final gulp. The wine burnt my throat as I swallowed. I felt my body sway slightly. Anaemia and alcohol were a bad combination. I felt the table hit my cheek before I realised that I was falling. Ben ran and cradled me gently. He rained soft kisses over my face and brushed my hair gently.

"It's ok," he tried to reassure me, "I'm here." He held my frail body and rocked me back and forth as though comforting a child. We both wept softly as the remnants of light drifted away and the darkness held us both in its embrace.

5

The following morning I was awoken by the sound of a coffee mug being placed on the bedside table. I looked up sleepily at Ben and smiled. For a moment I forgot. For a moment in my mind, I was still pregnant. As consciousness took hold the realisation of the truth came over me with a fresh wave of utter grief.

Tears were stinging my eyes.

"I forgot," I whispered to Ben hoarsely.

"Forgot what?" He asked gently.

"I forgot we lost him." I buried my head in the pillow and wept softly.

Ben gently cradled my shoulder and kissed my head.

For a moment he rested his head next to mine. Protectively he curled his body around mine.

"I'll be home late tonight." He spoke quietly, as though he was afraid to utter the words.

I nodded quietly. As he left me alone on the bed I cried once more. I allowed the grief to take over my body. I allowed myself to accept that the baby was gone.

I crept to the chest of drawers and pulled out the bottom drawer. Hidden underneath was my little treasure trove. A collection I had started when I had discovered I was pregnant.

Ben had said I should wait until my twelve-week scan to buy baby clothes, impatiently I had started to go shopping when I was alone. I hid my assortment of purchases. I took out a tiny hat and placed it on my knee. Gently I caressed it, imagining my baby wearing it. I closed my eyes and saw a pair of bright green eyes looking at me through my mind's eye.

I lifted the hat and brushed it gently against my cheek. The soft cotton weave felt luxurious. I gently kissed it, wishing desperately that my baby had grown big enough and strong enough to wear this hat and all of the other items that I had assembled.

I placed the hat back into its hiding place and hugged my knees. I rested my head against my arms and quietly cried.

If only we hadn't waited. If only I hadn't turned Ben down that night. If only.

I remembered sadly, the days following my thirtieth birthday.

~

Monday morning came with no word from Ben. I sat at my desk feeling empty. Waiting for him to call by teasing me, but he didn't arrive. By lunchtime I was distraught. I checked my phone every ten minutes.

"Is everything OK?" Derek asked as he passed by my desk.

"Mmm." I nodded, maybe in a bid to convince myself.

"It's funny." Derek mused knowingly. "Ben looks lost today too." My heart raced at the thought of Ben. I was angry, I was hurt, but I was terrified of losing his friendship.

"Go and talk to him," Derek suggested. My eyes filled up with tears. I turned away and started rooting under my desk for an imaginary pen.

"Hmm." I nodded again, unable to speak for fear of an eruption of tears.

Three days passed before I laid eyes on Ben. Each hour that passed was more painful than the one that went before. I longed for his comfortable friendship. In the evenings I sat with Maisy, stroking her fur spewing out my thoughts in a tangled mess. She didn't respond, only purred reassuringly.

On Thursday I was late for work. I'd lost my keys so couldn't lock up. I searched my flat, turning over all manner of items in my frenzied search. When I eventually found the keys I was half an hour late. I ran to the train station and jumped on the first train I could. I was out of breath by the time I reached the office. My face flushed with heat. My hair a tousled mess. The door to the lift was halfway closed when I darted into the reception.

"No!" I shouted at the door and launched myself in a desperate bid to stop the lift. I stumbled as I lurched forward, falling flat on my face. My arm managed to stop the lift door from closing. I crawled to my feet in an undignified mess and shuffled into the lift. The blood drained from my face as I came face to face with Ben. My eyes widened as a smile started to light up his green eyes.

"So, you haven't got any more co-ordinated over the past few days?" He smirked.

I gave him a steely stare, determined not to crack.

"Come on Hope." He pouted slightly. "I've really missed having you about, even though you have as much grace as a drunken elephant."

I turned my back so I faced the lift door. "You don't understand," I told him.

"You're right." He spoke with an angry tone to his voice. "I don't understand. You're my best friend. You're the last person I think of before I go to sleep and the first person I think of when I wake up."

I was shocked by his words. I had no idea that he felt this way. I glanced at him from the corner of my eye.

"Can I at least speak to your face Hope? Is that too much to ask?" Reluctantly I turned to face him.

"If I thought for one moment that it would damage our friendship I would never have kissed you." His eyes were full of sincerity. "I'm hurt that you thought I was just after a conquest though, I thought you knew me better than that."

"You've always got a different girl on the go, but they never last that long," I told him in my defence.

"I've dated three women in the time that I have known you!" He shook his head angrily. "What an utterly ridiculous comment, always exaggerating."

"Not one of those women has lasted more than a month." I spat the words at him.

"Ask yourself why." He shouted, storming out of the lift.

I stood there numb. I wanted to rewind to the moment I stumbled into the lift. I wanted to have the conversation again, but differently. I wanted him to wrap his arms around me. To give me assurances that he would never use me.

~

The days started to run into one another. Each day before Ben left for work he would ask me if I was going to come into the office that day. Each day I would reply with the same flat no. I started to crave my time alone. I found that alone I could grieve for the loss of my baby. When Ben was around I felt under pressure to behave as though everything was OK. I hated pretending. He had wanted me to pick myself up and dust myself off. I wanted that too, I really did, but I hurt so much. I couldn't just let go. I couldn't just forget. I felt cold and empty. I felt lost.

I spent my days in front of the TV. I forgot to eat or drink.

Weeks passed by. I hadn't noticed that I had lost so much weight until one morning I slipped on my jeans to find them loose and baggy. I looked in the mirror and saw that my face was gaunt. The dark circles beneath my eyes made me look like a living corpse.

"Hey beautiful." Ben placed a coffee down on my bedside table and kissed me lightly on the cheek. "What are you doing today?" I grimaced at the question. It felt like an intrusion, an accusation, an assumption that I would just sit around and cry again.

I shrugged. Unwilling to justify his assumptions.

"Maybe Monday would be a good time to get back to work?" He was trying to sound upbeat. "Derek was asking about the regeneration project you were working on. I think it would do you good to plough your energy back into it."

I glanced his way and shrugged again.

"It would be good to have a focus." I grimaced as he continued. "Get back to normal."

I bit my tongue.

"And in time, we can try again." With the words, I felt my body stiffen. I wondered how he could dismiss this baby so easily. I stared at him, mouth open, eyes glistening with tears.

"I need a shower." My words were flat and empty. I slammed the shower room door abruptly, locking the door behind me, barely holding back the floods of tears until the door was closed. My whole body heaved with the sobs.

Ben knocked on the bathroom door "Hope," his voice full of concern, "Hope I don't know how to do this, I don't know how to make it better."

"You can't" my voice was barely a whisper and I doubted he could hear me through the bathroom door. "Nobody can."

The days that followed were dark and desolate. I isolated myself inside my misery and refused to emerge from the black hole of my mind. I felt physically weak and mentally exhausted. I wanted to hide from my thoughts, I slept endlessly but even in the escape of my slumber, my dreams were blighted by the futility of me.

Guilt was my closest companion and I embraced it like a warm blanket. I snuggled in the warmth of the knowledge that I was to blame. I could barely stand the sight of Ben. His eternal optimism and need to remain positive infuriated me. I didn't want to be positive. I wanted to suffer. I wanted to feel the pain.

It felt wrong to just move on, to try again as though this baby had not existed, as though it had been a small glitch in an otherwise perfect plan. I cried every day until I had no tears left, then I would fall asleep in a heap of messy hair. My beautiful cottage steadily became more dishevelled. I rarely loaded the dishwasher, the washing basket overflowed and then spilt onto the bathroom floor.

I switched off my mobile for days at a time. Ben tried his best to crack my shell and find me in my lonely place but I pushed him away. I refused to be roused.

When he walked in from work I would see the look of disappointment on his face, seeing that another day had gone by and nothing had been achieved. The house was an unkempt mess and I knew that it frustrated him, but he tried to bite his tongue. I could see that he didn't look at me with the same adoring eyes, but I was too lost in myself to care. He would make suggestions to coax me back into normal life, but I refused to be drawn, his suggestions felt like instructions to me and they only served to make me determined not to dance to his tune.

"I am a strong independent woman" I had told him on one occasion, but even I knew that was no longer true. I was a shadow of my former self and that thought nagged in the recess of my brain. I could never bear to speak the words out loud but they were there in my unconsciousness and my dreams. My mother haunted my mind and it terrified me.

7

I sat in front of the TV wearing the same pyjamas I had worn for three days running. My hair a tangled mess, my eyes dark from all of the tears I had shed.

I felt empty now. A mere shell.

On the TV a toothless man called Ryan was sat between two equally toothless women, Cheryl and Sadie. The man was protesting his innocence to Cheryl while clearly hoping that Sadie wouldn't let him down. The look on her face suggested that she might.

I jumped up in shock as the sound of the doorbell interrupted my empty thoughts. I wasn't expecting a delivery. I shuffled to the door, making a cursory attempt to smooth my unkempt hair. I opened the door and peered through the gap. Eyes wide, I must have looked like something from a horror movie.

My eyes met Hayley's and I saw her expression change to one of complete shock. In her hand, she clutched a bunch of flowers. I scowled inwardly.

Within seconds her fake smile was plastered back onto her face.

"While you're ignoring my calls, I decided to come and see you in person." She stood before me like a demented Mary Poppins.

Clearly under the impression that she was here to restore joy and order into my otherwise messed up life. The very sight of her infuriated me. I inhaled deeply, fully aware that social convention stated that I ought to invite her in, but also conscious that the house wasn't fit for me to fester in, let alone to invite guests.

A half-smile twitched at the corners of my mouth, "I, err," I stumbled for words, trying to find a polite way to phrase the 'Fuck off' that was screaming through my mind.

"Why don't you go and get dressed and I'll put the kettle on?" She smiled in her pitying 'aren't I better than you?' way.

I wanted to protest, to tell her I was busy, that I wasn't ready for visitors, but I couldn't think of an excuse that she would accept. I reluctantly opened the door and let her through, secure in the knowledge that she would highlight the mess around my little cottage. I braced myself against the flurry of put-downs. I led her through to the conservatory, the least untidy room in the house. I moved the mugs that I had left on the window sill. As I scurried towards the bathroom, I gathered all manner of items in a futile attempt to tidy up the mess I had created over the previous weeks. "Pop the telly on, I'll be a couple of minutes" I called to Hayley as I headed upstairs.

The warm shower was like a comforting blanket. I found that the water cascading down my naked body soothed me, washing away my pain. I closed my eyes and tilted my face to meet the showerhead, letting the water rain down into the depths of my soul.

~

I remembered the day I met Hayley. It was Friday afternoon in September. The sun was bright and warm as I floated through the university campus as though I was in a foggy dream. I was still reeling from the death of my mother and the shock of having my whole world turned upside down. I had been on campus for a couple of weeks, so far there had been very few students around and I had managed to slip around mostly unnoticed. The head of campus had agreed that I could move in early due to 'exceptional circumstances'. I had scurried out for supplies. Freshers week was starting on Monday and the weekend would see the new intake of students descending upon campus in their droves. I wasn't ready to meet new people so had decided to stock up and hide away. I rushed away from the campus shop, bags in hand and Walkman on. Blur's "Parklife" blasting into my ears. I was oblivious to the world around me. I wasn't sure what I tripped on, but I did know that I fell to the ground with a thud. My precious supplies scattered all over the floor. I was thankful that there was nobody around to witness my literal fall from grace. I quickly gathered bread and beans. The batteries had popped out of my Walkman as I fell and I grabbed them and shoved them into the pocket of my leather biker jacket.

"Wow!" A shrill voice appeared from behind. Shocked I turned to face the owner of the voice. "That was quite a fall" she spoke in a clipped accent. She laughed loudly. "I hope you haven't broken anything."

"I'm fine," I replied quietly. I wanted the ground to open up and swallow me whole, yet this blond apparition persisted.

"Let me help you up." She offered her hand. I smiled, trying to appear grateful.

"I can manage," I smiled again as I rose to my feet. Shopping bags once again filled.

"I'm Hayley," she announced. I shrugged.

"I'm Hope." I looked at my feet awkwardly, partly because this unexpected social situation had been forced upon me, partly because to meet her eye would be a strain to my neck.

Hayley was tall and slender. Soft blond hair cut into what was commonly known as the 'Rachel' cut framed her heart-shaped face. Her face appeared to be perfectly symmetrical, her nose straight and slim regally sat in the middle of her face. Her bright blue, cat-like eyes almost appeared too big for her face. She was very striking, with the confident air of someone who had spent years of being admired everywhere she went. I felt foolish and awkward in comparison and could barely wait to get away.

"What a lovely name." She gushed. I shrugged with a half-smile again, unsure how to respond.

"Thanks for the…." I trailed off because I wasn't quite sure what I was thanking her for. She hadn't provided any real assistance, simply highlighted my embarrassment.

"We're all having a drink in the SU bar tomorrow night." I didn't know what to make of her announcement so I just smiled again. I was starting to feel a little like a gurning idiot.

"Meet us at eight." I shook my head vigorously, trying to find the words to voice my protest.

"You'll have a great time, do you know anyone yet?" I shook my head again.

"Ok, I'll come over to your halls and pick you up, where are you staying?" I wanted to refuse. I felt awkward and backed into a corner.

"Halifax building," I mumbled reluctantly.

"Oh yeah?" She smiled broadly. The Halifax building was part of the older, cheaper set of halls of residence at the University. I had managed to swing a single room but the rooms were very basic, offering little more than a bed, wardrobe and a desk. There were shared bathroom and kitchen facilities.

"I'm in the York building." Of course, she was.

The York building was a smart, newly built halls of residence. The rooms were plush and comfortable. They had fitted wardrobes, en-suite bathrooms and thick soft fitted carpets. The rooms cost almost double what mine cost. It was obvious that someone rather wealthy was payrolling her university stay.

She smiled once again in her overly sweet condescending way. "What's your room number? I'll pick you up at seven-forty-five."

"Eighteen." I reluctantly replied.

"Fab, see you tomorrow." She flashed that pearly white smile once more. "It'll be fantastic!" I didn't share her enthusiasm, but I smiled anyway.

~

Showered and dressed in my favourite jeans and a soft floral top. Reluctantly I admitted to myself that a fresh set of clothes and a sprinkling of make-up made me feel a little better. A little more like myself. I found Hayley in the kitchen.

“Hayley, leave those.” I protested as Hayley was putting the last of the dirty dishes in the dishwasher. Pots and pans were stacked on the draining board, surfaces were squeaky clean. The flowers that she had brought were proudly displayed in a vase in the window sill. I felt a stab of humiliation that Hayley had come into my home and cleared up my mess. Proud and independent, I wanted nothing from anyone. I knew that Hayley would have tutted over every cup, plate and crumb. I tried to tell myself that she was trying to help, but deep down I felt she was putting on a show. She wanted to prove what a wonderful, loyal and helpful friend she was.

The truth was that since our university days Hayley and I had been friends of sorts, but I always struggled with the relationship. I wasn’t sure if she knew how I felt or why I felt that way. She had a somewhat pitying, condescending manner and I often felt that she saw me as a pet project rather than a friend of equal standing. She had been there for me so many times throughout the years. She had helped me to brush myself off and climb back on the horse more times than I would care to mention, perhaps that was the problem. Perhaps I had allowed myself to become too vulnerable. Allowed her to take on that motherly role that had been lacking in so much of my life. Twenty-two years on from when we first met, I was growing tired of the power struggle and was desperate to change the dynamic, but maybe now was not the time. Maybe now I just needed to heel myself. Just the thought of heeling, of becoming myself again made me feel a stab of guilt.

"All done now!" She announced with a broad smile. I blushed, partly through shame, partly through anger.

"I don't expect anyone to clean up my mess," I told her, forcing myself to keep my tone light. We both knew that I wasn't just referring to the kitchen.

"That's what friends are for." She spoke more softly this time and I couldn't help to feel guilty for snapping.

I could feel my eyes stinging and a lump forming in my throat. I fought against the tears, angry with myself. I turned my face away from Hayley, pretending to busy myself with a smudge I had spotted on the window.

"Do you want to go to that little café down the road?" I wanted to get her out of the house, partly so I didn't have to have all of my mess on display and up for scrutiny, but partly because I had realised that I hadn't left the house for weeks. Now I was actually washed and dressed, I decided I might as well get out and about.

The café was set back from the road in a pretty little courtyard. Brightly coloured bunting hung from a pagoda. Climbing plants twisted in and out of the bunting with bursts of brightly coloured flowers spotted here and there.

We chose a seat in the sun. The sweet smell of honeysuckle filled the air and the hot sun warmed my pale skin.

"Could I have a latte please?" I asked the friendly, but slightly nervous young waitress when she arrived at our table, note pad in hand.

"Oh, could I have…" Hayley spoke in the very fake and exaggerated way that she reserved for those she considered to be her inferiors, "…a large mocha please, but," she held out her finger to show that she wasn't yet finished, "could you make sure it's foamy and could I have extra chocolate sprinkles?" The girl scribbled hurriedly on her pad.

She smiled nervously at Hayley, "Is that everything?"

"Yes, thank you."

Hayley turned to me before the waitress had left and asked loudly, "So, how are you?" I looked around at the tables in the vicinity, hoping that nobody else had been within earshot.

"Is that a silly question?" The expression on my face had once again given away my thoughts. I had never had a good poker face.

I shrugged. "I just never expected…." I trailed off, fighting tears once again. I felt foolish in a way. Foolish for being so deeply in love with a baby who had barely formed.

"Do you think it's because of your age." I knew full well that my age had more than likely been the biggest factor in the loss of my baby, but I felt angry with Hayley for speaking so bluntly.

I shrugged quietly.

"I'm not really looking for reasons," I lied. I had been searching for a reason my baby had died since the day of the scan. "I just wish….." I trailed off, we both knew what I wished. I wished I was sporting a growing baby bump. I wished that I could turn back the clock to before it had happened.

"Maybe you could get another cat." I stared at Hayley open-mouthed. I could barely believe that she had spoken such crass words out loud.

"I don't want a cat," I spoke softly. I smiled weakly, thinking of my cat Maisy.

"Anyway," I tried to appear cheerful and upbeat, "How are your two?"

Hayley had the perfect family. She had always had a plan in life and stuck to it like glue. After university, she had married her doctor boyfriend. They had a list of several countries on their bucket list that were ticked off before they settled down and had two children, a boy and then a girl in quick succession. A nanny had been employed to help take care of the children. The family bought a villa in the South of France, just to make sure they met every cliché you could think of.

Her offspring were now attending a private high school. There had been some concern about Joshua passing his exams and extra tuition had been drawn in to ensure that he got the marks. Joshua was a typical spoiled little rich kid. He had everything handed to him on a plate. He oozed confidence and arrogance in equal proportions. Hayley's daughter Clara was shy and subdued by comparison. She was sweet and pretty and instantly likeable, but Hayley rarely mentioned her sweet, unimposing daughter.

"They're doing well." Hayley smiled and nodding, happy to get on to her favourite subject. "Josh is captain of the rugby team. With his size and strength, he was, of course, the most obvious choice. David barely mentioned it to the coach and next thing you know he had made Josh captain." She sipped at her mocha and pulled a disapproving face, but carried on talking regardless. "He is working so hard at the moment, with his schoolwork, his rugby and then he is always out here or there with his friends, he is so popular, everyone wants to be his friend." She paused for breath, "I've told him that he needs to consider everyone though, that not everyone is as fortunate as him, he needs to make sure he spends time with those less fortunate than himself."

I nodded obediently, hoping that my eyebrow hadn't raised as obviously as I thought.

Eventually, Hayley and I parted. I promised to see her again soon, my head spinning with a range of emotions that I hadn't been ready to face.

I sat and reflected on my conversation with Hayley. I thought about her comment about my age. I felt angry with myself for not being more outspoken. I had of course given a great deal of thought to the cause of my miscarriage. The risks of miscarriage for older mums was well documented. The truth was that I would have loved to had a child when I was young, but that wasn't how it worked out.

9

I felt dizzy. The scent of pollen hung in the sea air. The sound of children laughing echoed around the clifftops from the beach below. The sight of a thousand swirling dancing butterflies filled the air, taunting me. Pulling me closer to the cliff edge, daring me to look. I resisted. Pulled back by the feeling of absolute dread. The sound of a deafening unearthly scream filled my ears and woke me sharply from my dream.

I sat up, sweat dripping from every pore. My heart was pounding in my chest. The realisation that I was dreaming did nothing to reassure me. Hot tears started to cascade down my cheeks. My body heaved silently through the tears. I was afraid of what it all meant. Ben stirred beside me. I needed him at that moment. I needed to feel safe. I was thankful for his presence for the first time in weeks.

"Hope?" he murmured through his sleep.

"I had a dream," I whispered hoarsely. I wondered if the feeling of dread was conveyed in my voice.

"What about?" He was a little more awake now.

"Butterflies." My reply was filled with foreboding. For me, butterflies held the same level of dread as an axe murderer. Most people would be in awe of their beauty, but for me butterflies were terrifying.

"I've told you before," Ben sat up beside me, reassuringly cupped my knee in his hand. "Butterflies can't hurt you. I don't know one other person who is afraid of butterflies." I began to sob.

He put his arms around me, held me close, his face nuzzled into my hair. I could feel his chest moving with every breath. His scent was reassuringly familiar. In his arms, I felt safe and protected from any demon real or imagined. My breathing slowed to match his. Our bodies pressed against one another. My cheek brushed against his. The warmth of his skin against mine felt delicious.

I brushed my lips lightly against his cheek. My fingers started to press against the muscles in his back, my fingertips explored his body in the darkness. His lips brushed against my neck, tingles gathered along my spine as endorphins flooded my body. My nipples ached to be touched, I parted my lips as my mouth reached for his. The pressure of his lips against mine was delicious. Gently, cautiously he started to undress me. His hand slipped under the vest top I wore and eased it up until my breasts were exposed. His lips found my left nipple. He sucked gently before his lips discovered my other nipple. I desired him, for the first time in weeks. My hand brushed gently against his naked thigh. I brushed my hand higher and higher until felt the familiar firmness that I longed for. Our lips merged as he lay me down against the bed. Skillfully he touched my body in the way only he understood. Our bodies merged as he pressed himself deeper inside me, moving rhythmically our bodies worked together to please one another. My fingertips pressed against his back as he pumped faster and harder, each movement brought a fresh wave of pleasure. My spine curved as I threw my head backwards and my body erupted in pleasure. We both groaned at the same time as our bodies succumbed to one another simultaneously. My nipples ached as I came, my heart pounded in my chest. As my breathing slowed calm serenity overcame me. I closed my eyes. Ben wrapped his arms around me, his lips brushing lovingly against my ear and my neck, his body pressed against my spine. I took his hand in mine. In that moment I felt safe and happy and loved more than any other. I wanted that moment to last forever.

I awoke from my slumber disappointed that I was no longer in Ben's arms. The feeling of closeness and contentment was still with me. I longed for his lips to touch mine. The room was flooded with light. Ben stood in front of the mirror of my dressing table tweaking his hair this way and that. I focussed on his strong cheekbones and his soft lips. His trousers were tight against his firm buttocks. I wanted to touch him. I wanted him to touch me. He noticed me watching him, a smile started to play with the corners of his mouth.

"What are you doing today?" Ben sat on the bed next to me. He hadn't asked that question for a while, probably because he knew the answer was the same. I had no plans. I would get out of bed for around lunchtime, just in time to slump in front of the TV with a coffee until about 4 pm. I then planned to rush up for a shower just prior to Ben coming home so I could pretend I was feeling better.

I shrugged.

"Why don't you meet up with Hayley again?" I raised my eyebrows at Ben's question.

"That's all you've got?" I turned my back to him, angry that he had brought her up. I had told him of her visit the previous week. Told him about her audacity at cleaning the kitchen, about her insistence that I needed to get a cat and give up the idea of having a child of my own.

"Hope," Ben spoke softly, "the whole world isn't against you."

"For Christ sake Ben," I spoke angrily, but I wasn't quite sure why. "You know how I feel about Hayley." I sat up and looked him in the eye.

"Sure, she's a pain in the arse," he smiled, "but she's not all bad. You've been friends for years."

"Friends don't tell you how to live your life."

"Are you sure that's what she's doing?"

"You just don't get it."

"Maybe I do though!" This time his voice was raised. "Maybe I do get it. I get that you're rolling around in self-pity and you're looking for someone to blame, someone to lash out at so you don't have to look at yourself."

"What the fuck Ben?" I felt as though he had smacked me in the face, wounded by his words.

"You're not the only one who is hurting Hope." His voice began to crack as he spoke. "You're not the only one who lost a baby that day, but some of us have to go on. Continue to put one foot in front of the other and just get on with life."

"You're a shit when you want to be." My eyes narrowed in an attempt to push away the tears.

"Here we go." He stood up angrily, grabbing his wallet from the bedside table. "Lash out some more, see if it makes you feel better." His jaw tensed as he looked me in the eye. "Just when I thought we were getting somewhere, just when I thought you could show some affection."

"You mean when you thought you could start getting your end away again?" I spat the words angrily, hatefully. Sad that I was taking the love we had shared last night and shredding it before my eyes.

"Yeah, because that's all I want," Ben spoke harshly, sarcastically. "I don't want to express my love for you, I just want someone to fuck." He shook his head angrily. "If I just wanted sex then there are far easier ways to go about it than this." He looked around at the unkempt bedroom. Piles of washing, make-up, towels half-read books all around. At that moment I caught a glimpse of myself in the mirror. Makeup smudged around my eyes, hair a tangled mess. My eyes looked deep and dark and hollow. If the eyes were truly the windows to the soul mine were in need of some maintenance.

I lay down on the bed and began to cry. Ben walked out of the room without looking back to say goodbye.

10

I heard Ben shuffling around downstairs. It had been a week since our fight. We had spoken in fits and starts. He had offered me coffee, I had asked what he wanted for dinner. He told me briefly about his day, complained about Carol from reception and some mix up with her computer system. We had not been close, not since the night of my dream. I harboured resentment towards him that I could not shake, maybe in part because I knew he was right. I was suffocating in self-pity. He may have been able to forget the child we had dearly wanted, but for me that was impossible.

Ben appeared at the bedroom door. Tray in hand, dressed in my dressing-gown. I was shocked at first to see him stood there.

"Happy Birthday." He spoke softly and kissed my head tentatively as he placed the tray down on the bed.

"Oh." I couldn't hide the shock. On the tray sat a plate of perfectly cooked eggs benedict, a pot of tea, a glass of champagne and an envelope with the word Hope handwritten across the middle in Ben's neatest handwriting. He had turned the o into a heart shape, I smiled at the corniness of the gesture, but rather pleased at the same time. "Thank you," I couldn't help but smile.

I opened the card. On the front there was a drawing of a pretty young couple sat under a tree. He was sat with his back against the trunk of the tree and she was sat leaning against him, head tilted backwards and gazing into his eyes. On the ground were the remnants of a picnic. A tall wine bottle stood half-empty, each of them held a wine glass. The image was more than slightly reminiscent of one of our early dates. Ben and I had visited the Lake District for a weekend away. We had taken a picnic out in the sunshine and sat under a tree drinking wine, eating all manner of cheeses and kissing like a pair of teenagers. We had attracted far too much attention from the other tourists, but we didn't care. We were enjoying the excitement and passion of discovering one another. Seeing the image made me smile. I was pretty confident that Ben had chosen that card specifically because it also reminded him of that day. "To my Wife on Your Birthday" was printed at the top of the card.

Inside the printed words read "I love you more today than I did yesterday. Tomorrow I will love you more than I do today."

Ben's handwriting read "To my Hope, Life begins at.......... You. You are my love, you are my world, you are my Hope for the future."

Inside the card was a second envelope. I opened the envelope and took out a second card, this one held a spa voucher. Again, Ben had penned a message.

"Hope, you are always beautiful to me, but to help you to feel beautiful inside I have booked two days of relaxation and treats for you to enjoy."

The voucher was for a day at a Spa for two people, followed by afternoon tea, an overnight stay including dinner and drinks then a personal shopping session and makeover on day two. I was a little overwhelmed at the gesture. It seemed so unlike Ben to think of such a lovely gift, but then it seemed so unlike any man to be fair.

"Wow!" was all I could manage as I took a sip of the champagne. "When are we going to book it for then?"

"I've booked it." He smiled as he replied. "For today."

I checked the time on my phone in a panic, it was seven-thirty. "Bloody hell! What time for?"

"It's for ten am, Hayley, is going to pick you up at nine."

"Hayley?" I couldn't believe he had done it again. "I thought you would want to come."

"It's a bit girly," he cringed slightly, "Even for someone as in touch with their feminine side as me."

"But Hayley?" I raised my eyebrows.

"Who else would you take Hope?" I wracked my brains for the name of another female friend but came up with nothing.

"You'll have fun." He tried to reassure me. "She's a pain in the arse at times, but she's not that bad." I began to wonder when Ben had altered his view of Hayley.

"I can't believe I'm forty." I pulled my face.

"Neither can anyone else," Ben remarked, "you look amazing."

I pulled my face again.

"I mean it," he told me, "you really do. You're so beautiful Hope."

I smiled. I wished I could believe it. I had never felt beautiful. I'd always felt as though I wasn't quite good enough. When Ben and I had first got together those feelings had subsided. He had been so wonderful and supportive. He had admired me in a way that I didn't understand. He had made me feel sexy, confident and desired. I wondered if a weekend away was just what I needed. A way to blow away the cobwebs and feel desirable once more.

"Thank you." I smiled and kissed him gently on the cheek. "I'd forgotten all about my birthday."

"Really?" He raised his eyebrows and looked at me with mock puzzlement.

"Well, sort of," I smiled again, a little embarrassed.

The truth was that I had wanted to forget my birthday. I had wanted it to pass by without too much of a mention, but I was secretly thrilled that Ben had taken the time to book a special day for me, even if I was to spend it with Hayley.

"Helen died when she was forty." My thoughts turned into words before I could stop them.

Ben looked shocked. I had told him very little about my mother, only that she had died.

"How did she die?" He asked gently.

I shook my head. "I don't want to talk about it, I shouldn't have mentioned her."

"She was your mother," he hugged me gently as he spoke, "it's good to talk."

I shook my head again.

"When you're ready, when you want to talk about it, I'm here."

I nodded in thanks. Ben wanted to know more. I wasn't sure I would ever be ready to talk about my mother though. Some memories are too painful.

11

As promised Hayley arrived to collect me at nine am. I was a little apprehensive about spending the weekend with her but was thankful that we would be tucked away in the spa all day, away from prying eyes.

Hayley flashed me a reassuring smile as I jumped in her car. “I can’t believe Ben has done all of this!” She exclaimed. “He thinks the world of you, you know that?” I felt a stab of guilt about my treatment of Ben over the previous few weeks.

Hayley was right, Ben did think the world of me. Over the past few weeks, I had forgotten how much we cared about each other. I had isolated myself from everything. I was punishing myself for the loss of my baby.

“You’re right.” I nodded in agreement. “I’ve never been to one of these before,” I added nervously, referring to the spa.

Hayley was an old hand when it came to beauty treatments. Hayley and her husband David often entertained his doctor friends at their home and Hayley had to make sure she looked the part. Unlike me, her nails were always manicured, her eyebrows always shaped and her hair was always perfect. I suspected that she treated herself to the occasional Botox session, but neither of us would ever mention that.

“It’ll be fun.” She smiled. I hoped she was right.

My heart skipped a beat when Hayley pulled into the car park of the hotel. The hotel was an imposing three-story Georgian building set in beautiful, immaculately kept grounds. The door to the reception was framed by an arbour, decorated with fairy lights and covered with climbing plants that were in full blossom. To the right, a large lawn was home to a magnificent weeping willow. Pretty lanterns of all different shapes and sizes had been hung from the branches. Stones crunched beneath our feet as Hayley and I followed the gravel path to the reception door.

We were greeted by a pretty girl with a bright smile and red hair. As Hayley booked in, I gazed around in awe. The attention to detail was impressive. The walls were decorated with bright floral wallpaper. Paintings of landscapes adorned the walls. My eye caught a striking painting of a small child with soft blonde curls. Her eyes gleamed with joy as she held a picked daisy in her chubby hand. The child stood in a meadow full of tall grass and wildflowers. I could almost smell the scent of the flowers as I gazed at the image, it was so beautifully familiar. Part of me wanted to hug that child, tell her she was safe, she was loved.

"Come on Birthday girl." Hayley's voice broke my focus on the painting. I turned to look at her, she had two fluffy white dressing gowns draped over her arm and a bottle of champagne in the other hand. "I didn't think you liked dogs." I looked at her with a furrowed brow, then gazed back towards the painting that had captivated my attention. The painting was of a wild meadow. In the centre of the painting an afghan hound sitting majestically amongst the tall grass. I turned away and followed Hayley, baffled. I looked at the bottle in her hand. "I'm not sure I should have any more champagne."

I wasn't sure what to expect. Hayley took charge in her typical fashion. I was happy that I didn't have to think too hard. We dropped off our belongings in our room then headed to the spa.

We entered a small room that was home to two white leather sofas and a white gloss coffee table. A white cabinet stood against the wall with a coffee machine stood on top. There were all different types of pods to create any type of tea or coffee that you might desire. There were four oak doors marked "Treatment Room". Hayley had booked a variety of treatments, starting with a full wax. A stout beautician appeared from within one of the treatment rooms and called my name in a strong Scottish accent. I stood apprehensively and gazed at Hayley for support, she just smiled and said: "catch you at lunchtime."

"Strip down, put on the robe and sit yerself on the treatment bed." The beautician ordered as we entered the stark white treatment room. The whale music playing on the CD player did nothing to relax me.

I looked around for somewhere private to undress, there was a treatment bed that reminded me of a doctors surgery, there were three trolleys loaded with a variety of equipment, most of it was completely alien to me. There was nowhere to hide my modesty while I changed. I threw the robe over my arm, "Is there somewhere I could err……." I looked helplessly towards the beautician.

She was immaculately preened. Her hair was neatly held in a tight bun. She wore a pristine tunic and white trousers. I wanted to call her Nurse Rosetta, but her badge said Cat so I thought I should stick with that. Her face was perfectly made up, but she had no softness to her expression. She was imposing, stern and more than a little intimidating.

"I'll nip outside fer yer." She informed me. "I'll grab you a glass of that Champers yer mate had too cos yer look like yer might need it." I relaxed slightly as she spoke.

"Thank you." I smiled as she slipped out of the room.

Quickly I stripped down to my underwear and threw the gown on over the top. I heard a sharp rap on the door, "are yer done Chick?" Cat enquired.

"Yes," I called back, "Thank you."

She adjusted the backrest of the treatment bed and checked I was comfortable. I was starting to relax. "We'll start with the legs." She walked over to one of the trolleys and started to stir the wax. I was fascinated by all of the equipment and bottles and boxes. I had no idea that looking good required so much stuff.

Cat smeared the wax onto my shin with a wooden spatula. The gooey liquid was warm and comforting as it was spread over my skin. She pressed a paper sheet over the wax, taking care to press it down firmly. Before I could even begin to brace myself for what might come next, the sheet and the wax and what felt like half my leg were gone. I let out a scream.

"Arch come on, ney bother." Cat looked at me with disappointment in her eyes. "It came off clean, canny have hurt a jot." A smile played with the corners of her mouth, "wait until we get on to the bikini wax!" My eyes grew wider as I gulped a mouthful of champagne.

12

By lunchtime, I was red raw. My skin tingled in pain, but I was surprisingly smooth. I repeatedly brushed my hand down my shin to feel the softness of my hair-free skin.

I was reminded of my first shaving experience when I had borrowed Helen's razor and removed most of my bodily hair and several chunks of skin. I could visualise Helen and her shock as she inspected my tattered legs, tutting as she scolded me for using her razor, sticking bits of tissue over the cuts to stop the bleeding.

Lunch was afternoon tea in our room.

When we first arrived at the room we had quickly opened the door and thrown our bags down on one of the beds. We had barely taken the time to inspect the room.

It was a large room, beautifully decorated. There were two king-sized beds, one on either side of the room. The walls were covered with the same floral print that had been used in the rest of the hotel. Several pretty paintings hung on the walls. There was a table and two ornate high backed chairs sat in front of a large French window framed by soft, white silk curtains. The window opened up onto a small balcony that overlooked the garden. A wishing well stood in the middle of a neat lawn. The lawn was framed by flower beds that were full of colour and life. I watched as a bee busied himself buzzing from one flower to the next. Nervously I stood back from the window and planted myself on one of the chairs. I was pretty sure I had seen butterflies down there. I had a nervous feeling in the pit of my stomach.

I had quite an appetite by the time the waiter arrived with our tea.

An antique cake stand was placed in the centre of the table. Neat little sandwiches were lined up like soldiers, huge scones filled with cream and jam sat on the next layer, the top layer was adorned with all manner of cakes and treats, from the classic Victoria sponge to an Eton mess.

A silver teapot and milk jug were placed next to the stand. The china teacups and saucers reminded me of Jo-Jo and I smiled fondly. A sugar bowl held sugar cubes and a set of silver tongues.

We were next presented with two champagne glasses. The waiter poured a little from the bottle, waited for me to taste the liquid and signal my approval before filling both glasses.

"Wow." I smiled at Hayley. "This is nice." She returned my smile and nodded.

"How was this morning?" She asked.

"Oh my God!" I exclaimed. "I have never felt pain like it!" I knew I was exaggerating but felt the need to be overdramatic.

"I thought doing my legs was bad enough, but then the eyebrows. Then she did my tash, then you know….."

Hayley just laughed.

"I don't know what you're laughing at." My eyes narrowed as I looked at her, but we both knew I wasn't really cross.

"I like it though," I mused, brushing my shin once more, "not the sheer agony of every hair on my body ripped out, but I feel so smooth."

"Ben's going to love it." Hayley winked at me. I laughed bashfully.

"We've not really been physical," I mumbled, but Hayley heard and nodded. "I just feel so shitty about everything." I looked her in the eye. "I've been lashing out at Ben, as though it's all his fault and I know it's not fair…." I trailed off.

"That's what people do." She spoke softly. "I'm sure he understands, I know he just wants to help."

"I just don't feel the same," I confessed quietly, I then shrugged as the thought was too awful to bear. "I don't feel the same about anything to be fair."

I was admitting my feelings for the first time, partly to Hayley, but mostly to myself. Half-formed thoughts were spewing from my lips in a slightly incoherent jumble.

"I got so carried away with the idea of being a Mum, it became the most important thing to me in the world." Tears started to form in the corners of my eyes, "now the idea of being pregnant terrifies me."

"I understand." She spoke softly, she rested her hand on mine to comfort me.

"I look at Ben and I just can't remember why I loved him. It's like I was a different person then. It's as though," I shook my head and shrugged, "I'm talking shit, it doesn't matter."

"You're not talking shit, Hope." She spoke sternly. "We have been friends for more than twenty years. In all of that time, I have felt like I never knew the real you. You show people what you want them to see. For once you're being honest and talking about the stuff that you normally keep so well hidden, don't hold back because you're afraid."

We sat in silence for a moment. Hayley's hand still resting on mine in an awkward gesture that was intended to give comfort.

I thought about what she had said, about keeping things hidden.

Hayley was right. I did keep things hidden. I never talked about my life before I started university. I never talked about my mother or Port Merdow or Jo-Jo.

Hayley had no secrets or hidden past. Her family were very much a part of her life. Over the years Hayley's family home had been a hub where we would meet before nights out, where we would go for parties or just where Hayley and I would hang out with Hayley's mum.

Hayley didn't have any painful memories in her past. Her childhood had been very privileged and very happy. Her father was a very successful property owner, even before owning property became popular. Both her parents had worked hard to build a successful business but had managed to always make sure they had time for Hayley and her younger sister.

In Hayley's life, everything was perfect. She always presented herself that way. She was always positive. If she had a bad day or if things weren't going to plan, I was pretty sure she wouldn't tell anyone because that would mean ruining the illusion of perfection. I decided that everyone kept things hidden. Why should I be any different?

"I'm just a bit pissed." I laughed, taking a gulp of the champagne, "We came here to celebrate my Birthday and have a laugh. I think what I need right now is to just forget everything, to focus on being happy."

I lifted the bottle and emptied the last drops of champagne into mine and Hayley's glasses. I then lifted my glass.

"To being forty." I toasted. Hayley joined me in the toast.

13

After lunch, Hayley and I staggered back to the treatment rooms. Hayley had to stop me from falling along the way. I felt like a rebellious teenager who had been drinking before the school disco. I was just waiting for one of the teachers to discover my secret. Inside the waiting area, I sat in mock sobriety waiting for my afternoon treatments.

"Oh my god!" I whispered to Hayley in an exaggerated hushed voice. "I think that champers has gone to my head a bit."

"Do you think?" She asked sarcastically, laughing.

"Yeah," I slurred my words, hardly noticing her sarcasm.

"Hope?" A soft voice enquired. I looked up in a daze.

"Yes," I answered keenly.

"Would you like to come this way for your massage?"

I followed the meek-looking masseuse to the treatment room.

"My name is Sandy, I've got you down for a massage and a facial. If you just take off your robe, you'll be better in just knickers, then lay yourself facedown." She smiled welcomingly. I was pretty sure she could sense my nervousness. "I'll just need to grab some oils from the storeroom"

The room was warm, when I took off my fluffy robe I felt exposed even though I was alone in the room. I obediently took off my bra and laid myself down on the massage table, laughing to myself as I rested my face against the face rest. It reminded me of a joke the kids would tell at primary school about a fat kid stuck in a lift. My cheeks seemed to squish towards my nose. There was a towel on the bed and I laid it over my bottom to protect my modesty.

I had never had a massage. The idea of being touched in what would appear to be a rather intimate way made me nervous. I was the type of person who valued personal space.

"Ah, you're all ready." Sandy returned with several bottles of lotion in her hands.

"I've got some Chamomile oil," she informed me, "it'll help to relax you, ease all that tension." I wondered if it was that obvious that I was so tense. I looked up from the face rest and smiled at her, trying too hard to appear relaxed.

"We'll start with the arms." She took hold of my left arm, rather firmly and started to rub the oil into my skin. The motion was soothing and relaxing. As she worked around my body; from my arms to my legs, to my shoulders, I felt my pain floating away. My thoughts seemed to leave me. My focus was purely on the movement of hands and the release of pressure. Slowly I drifted into another world.

In my dream, I was my three-year-old self. I was sat, legs crossed on a picnic blanket. The picnic blanket held a pretty china tea set that I remembered vividly from my childhood. Matching pink flowers adorned each of the cups. In front of me was Faith, a china cup in her chubby hand. I felt the blood drain from my face as I was faced with her image. Blonde curls held in pigtails. Soft pink lips curled into a warm smile. Faith looked so pretty, so happy.

"Where have you been?" I asked, barely able to keep the sadness from my voice.

"I had to go." She replied, her voice was mine, yet eerie and distant, like an animated ventriloquist puppet.

"But why did you go?"

"You know the answer," I felt goosebumps all over my body as she spoke with my voice. "you know how to find the truth."

I snapped from my dream with a start. I felt chilled to the core. I had forgotten about the imaginary friend of my childhood. To be faced with such a realistic image of my make-believe doppelganger uneased me. I could feel my heart pounding in my chest. I felt dizzy and disorientated. I raised my head to find myself alone in the treatment room. Sandy must have slipped out of the room when I drifted off to sleep. I sat up with a start, but my slippery body had no purchase on the PVC bed. I felt my body slipping but nothing I did in my dreamlike state seemed to help to correct my balance. I came crashing down onto the hard floor, my head hitting the legs of the massage table as I fell. The door suddenly swung open and there stood Sandy and Hayley. I hurriedly grabbed for my robe in a bid to hide my nudity.

"What on earth Hope?" Exclaimed Hayley, her voice ringing with laughter. "You little drunkard, falling asleep during a massage, then falling off the table." She laughed loudly again. "You're so funny." She told me.

I stared at her, with eyes wide. I was still disorientated from my dream. I was haunted by the words I had spoken through Faith's lips.

"I, uh." I started to speak, unsure what I wanted to say. I wanted to defend myself. Explain that it wasn't the wine, but I knew she would just bulldoze over my words. I stopped. I awkwardly wrapped the robe around me and climbed to my feet.

"Let's go for a sauna, see if we can clear that head." Hayley smiled and linked my arm.

I obediently followed Hayley's lead, resentment starting to build.

14

I managed to shake my dreamlike state by the time we reached the pool area. We had stopped to change into swimwear along the way. We found two loungers in a central location and disrobed. I wore a full swimsuit, plain black in colour. Hayley wore a bright pink bikini, tied at the sides with string. Her bosom was spilling out of the top. She was eliciting sideways glances from men and women alike. Her hourglass figure the focus of attention.

"Sauna." She announced, seemingly oblivious to the attention she was drawing from all corners. I nodded and followed.

The heat from the sauna hit me as soon as I opened the door.

The small, dimly lit room was empty. Hayley and I sat at the far end of the sauna. I watched the steam as it formed patterns, dispersed by the hazy light. I could feel sweat forming on my back and dripping down my spine. I was thankful that Hayley and I were the only ones in the sauna, it seemed too small a space to share.

"How was your massage?" Hayley awkwardly filled the silence.

"Surprisingly good," I admitted. "Really relaxing."

"Yeah, you fell asleep!" She laughed.

I nodded, recalling my strange dream with the lifelike image of my imaginary friend. I figured that Faith was my projection of myself. That the dream was some metaphor from my past. Whatever the reason, I found it disconcerting.

"Do you think dreams have meanings?" I asked absentmindedly.

"Not sure," she replied, "I think they're probably just your minds way of processing the day."

"Hmmm," I mumbled thoughtfully.

"Room for a little one?" Asked a gruff voice as the door swung open. The doorway was blocked by an oafish figure with a towel wrapped around his ample waist. He sat himself down, legs spread wide apart, resting himself against the wall. My eyes widened as I caught sight of his testicle hanging down from the edge of the bench.

Suddenly the sauna felt much smaller. I moved closer to Hayley in order to move farther away from the man.

Sweat started to form in beads on his shining bald head. I suddenly felt dizzy and claustrophobic. I wanted to escape but the man was blocking the doorway.

"Where are you two ladies from?" He enquired in an attempt to make polite conversation. He did nothing to ease my discomfort.

"Err, we're kind of local." I ventured, not wanting to give too much away.

"We're from Chester." I glared at Hayley as she answered with complete honesty. "Well Hope is from Bristol as you can probably tell from her accent, but we both live in Chester. I was brought up there."

"Chester is a lovely city." He nodded as he spoke. "It's not what it used to be, but what do you expect now the Romans have gone?" He laughed at his own joke.

I was stunned to hear Hayley laughing along. I didn't want to make polite conversation with a man exposing his testicles. I wanted to get out of the sauna, to run away. I wanted to go home to Ben. In my mind I imagined me recalling the events of the day to Ben. How he would listen intently. How he would nod and smile and laugh in the right places. In that moment I felt a wave of affection for my husband that I had not felt for weeks.

"I'm from Burnley," he ventured without being asked, "I'm over here on a bit of business, stopping here for a couple of nights before I go back over."

Hayley nodded politely.

"We're here for a bit of R and R," Hayley told him. "It's Hope's fortieth, her husband booked us a spa weekend, he's such a catch." I was starting to feel very uneasy.

Hayley was being rather flirty that I found difficult to understand. She was giving away far too much information.

"Fortieth hey?" he shifted on his seat as he spoke, exposing the other testicle. "It's mine next year, dreading the bloody thing." I could barely believe he was under fifty, let alone forty.

Again, Ben came to mind. His youthful looks and trim body. At forty-two, Ben looked a good ten years younger than Hayley's new friend.

"You're nowhere near forty!" Hayley's voice seemed utterly false in my ears. I couldn't understand her thought process at all. Why on earth was she stroking this man's ego?

"Ha, I wish." He chuckled to himself, clearly enjoying the attention. "What are you girls doing for dinner this evening?"

"I think we're just eating here at the hotel," Hayley told him.

"I have a booking for La Vie Da Paris, I'll give them a call and tell them to expect three."

"Oh, how on Earth did you get a booking there?" Hayley gushed.

"It's not what you know…." He trailed off.

"We couldn't possibly afford to eat there," Hayley told him in an utterly flirtatious way.

"Oh, It's my treat. I'll be glad of company," he replied, "these business trips can get proper lonely." My eyes widened as he spoke.

He wasn't looking for the kind of company I was willing to be party to. The heat was going to my head. I was dizzy and nauseated. The thought of spending an evening with this loathsome man just to experience fine dining was a step too far. I stood up and started to walk towards the door. My voice was stern as it left my lips.

"Thank you for the offer," I tried not to touch his knees as I manoeuvred myself out of the door. I stood in the doorway looking back at Hayley who remained seated. "My husband booked this spa break for Hayley and I. He booked an afternoon tea for us which was beautiful, he's booked an evening meal for us in the restaurant here too. He didn't book it so we could spend the evening elsewhere with people we don't know. He booked it because he recognised that I needed a change of scenery. I needed to feel special, but you know what?" I directly at Hayley as I spoke. "The times that I feel most special, the only time I have ever felt special, is when I'm with Ben."

I turned on my heels and stormed out of the sauna. I grabbed my robe without looking back and headed straight for the hotel room.

Back in the room, I sat on the bad, waiting for Hayley to come marching into the room. When she hadn't arrived after ten minutes, I picked up my phone. I went to messages and clicked the new message button. I started to type her name then selected her from the list of contacts.

"Where are you?" I typed but paused before hitting send. I was angry with her for encouraging the man. He had made me feel uneasy. I had no idea what his intentions were, but she was an adult. She had got along just fine up until this stage in her life without me checking up on her every move. I deleted the message then started again, this time choosing Ben as my contact. "I miss you." I typed but deleted it. "I'm frightened." Again I deleted the message. "Hi." Third time lucky. I sent the message this time.

I sat and waited for a reply. Fifteen minutes went by and still, there was no sign of Hayley and there was no reply from Ben.

I threw the phone down on the bed and decided to run a bath.

15

"Hope?" I heard Hayley's voice through the bathroom door. The water was cold. I looked at the tips of my fingers, the deep wrinkles told me that I had been in the bath for quite some time. I had not noticed drifting off to sleep. I was thankful that this time I had not been troubled by cryptic dreams.

"Where the hell have you been?" I asked angrily, pulling myself up out of the cold water and wrapping a towel around me. I opened the bathroom door, prepared to confront her angrily. I was shocked to see the oaf stood next to her. My jaw dropped. I slammed the bathroom door in a swift angry motion.

"I'll catch you in the bar." I heard Hayley telling him in a flirtatious tone. As I heard the door shut, I flung the bathroom door open once more.

"What the hell are you playing at Hayley?" I shouted the words louder than I had intended.

She laughed "Oh, calm down Hope, for God's sake. We're supposed to be having fun." I glared at her.

"That guy isn't going to want the kind of fun that we were hoping for! That guy is looking for a couple of escorts for the night!"

"He's lonely." She argued. "And that restaurant is supposed to be amazing."

"This was supposed to be amazing." I motioned to the room, but we both knew I meant the whole weekend.

Ben and I were financially comfortable, but we weren't rich by any stretch of the imagination. A weekend like this must have cost more than we could afford. It felt so wrong not to be making the absolute most of it. Spending any time massaging the ego of any man seemed a complete betrayal to Ben.

"And it's lovely," she agreed, "but it's not La Vie Da Paris."

"Jesus Hayley!" I threw my hands in the air in disbelief. "What do you think that guy is going to want in return for dinner?" I didn't give her chance to speak. "He's not just looking for polite conversation for the evening!"

"Well, maybe I'm looking for more than that too!" Her words shocked me.

"What the fuck? What about David?" I pictured her mild-mannered husband with his potbelly and receding hairline. His utter devotion to Hayley and the children. I could imagine how hurt he would be to hear her speak such words.

"David?" She spat his name. "Like David gives a fuck! David's banging his secretary!"

I stopped in stunned silence, mouth wide open.

"What?" was all I managed.

"Yeah, absolute cliché, right?" Tears started to roll down her face. I stared at her in disbelief.

"What?" I repeated. This time softer. "Are you sure? Since when? How do you know?"

We both sat on our respective beds.

"I've suspected for a while." She spoke softly after a long sigh. "He started to dress better, you know. Instead of Burton, he started dressing at Hollister, Super Dry, and Hugo Boss. He went on a diet, joined the gym. He started to buy aftershave every time we went anywhere. Stopped going for a trim at his usual barbers and started to go to the designer hairstylist on the high-street."

I wanted to say that didn't mean anything, that wasn't proof of an affair. It's difficult when you start to realise you're not as young as you were. To me it sounded like a classic midlife crisis, all that was missing was the sports car.

I sat in silence waiting for Hayley. I wanted her to decide when she was ready to speak.

"He would ask me what I thought a lot, like did he look ok." She pulled her face. "I never quite knew what to say. I figured it was a midlife crisis. None of us like getting any older, I've had a bit of Botox." Her confession surprised me.

"One day I was sorting through washing. There were a load of papers in David's back pocket. I pulled them out," her face contorted into disgust, "there was a condom!"

I knew that Hayley had her tubes tied after her daughter had been born. I had been quite defensive of her at the time. I had felt that as the procedure was so much simpler for a man, David ought to be the one who had the operation.

"So what makes you so sure it's the secretary?" I pressed gently. "or that there wasn't some innocent explanation?"

"I bugged his phone." She confessed. I was stunned. I didn't even know that Hayley had any idea how to do that. She would have been furious if it had been the other way around. "It was all there. Flirty texts, arrangements to meet up, dick pick the works." She shook her head angrily through the tears. "It turns out that he'd been meeting up with her when he took Josh for rugby practice."

"Does he know that you know?" I didn't know what else to say.

She shook her head. "Utterly oblivious." Her voice was filled with disgust. "He must think I'm stupid."

"What are you going to do?" It seemed like a stupid question. In my mind, the only option was to kick him out and file for divorce.

"I don't know," she shrugged, "I've been wondering that myself." Fresh tears started to roll down her cheeks. Her shoulders heaved with the sobs that wracked her body.

"Well, I'll tell you one thing," I walked over and sat next to her on her bed. I wrapped my arms around her slim frame, "hooking up with that creep from the sauna really isn't going to help."

"I don't think I'd have gone through with anything," she confessed, "I think I just wanted someone to notice me."

"Hayley!" I exclaimed. "In that bikini everyone noticed you. Half the women would have taken you to bed, let alone the men."

Hayley appeared bashful. I realised just how much her ego had been bashed because of David's indiscretion.

"If David has been cheating then he's a fool." I looked at her directly in the eye. "Do you want to leave him?"

She shook her head tearfully. "How can I? I'm nothing without him." Her words shocked me.

"Don't you ever believe that for one second!" I demanded. "You couldn't be nothing if you tried. Just look at the way everyone gravitates to you whenever you're around."

She shrugged.

"Look, you don't have to make any decisions tonight except one." I looked at her sternly. "The only decision you need to make tonight is to tell creep features that you're not interested."

"Oh, I forgot about him." She started sobbing again.

"You get showered and changed for dinner," I told her. "I'll get dressed and I'll go and tell him you're not well. What's his name?"

"Alan." She whispered coyly.

I nodded.

Down in the bar area, I spotted Alan straight away. He had already latched on to somebody new. A leggy redhead stood looking at him, laughing in the right places and smiling in an over-enthusiastic manner. Her ample bosom was resting on the bar, jiggling as she laughed. Alan couldn't take his eyes off her breasts. Just looking at him made me want to bathe in bleach, I felt that unclean. I shrugged to myself thinking that I needn't have worried about making excuses for Hayley, she wasn't going to be missed. As I turned on my heels, I heard a screech of distaste. I turned back to see the redhead angrily chastising Alan. He grabbed her buttocks with one hand and rested the other on her shoulder, eyes firmly glued to her breasts. "Calm down love. It's just a bit of fun."

I'm not sure if it was the wine or listening to a heartbroken Hayley recounting the sorrow of finding that David had been taking care of his secretary. Whatever the cause I was incensed. I turned back on my heels and stormed over to Alan, without a plan I had to improvise.

"Here you are!" I shouted at him angrily. "And who is this now? Your next conquest?"

"Look, love...." Alan started to protest.

"Don't 'Love' me! What am I supposed to tell the children about their father and his extra-curricular activities?"

"You have kids?" The redhead stepped backwards in disgust.

"And on our wedding anniversary, you decide to treat me this way? I just went for a shower and I come back to find this?"

"You what?" Clearly what I had said struck a chord, but I wasn't finished yet. I could tell that we were drawing lots of attention, but I carried on.

"And don't you think of coming anywhere near me until you've sorted out your little pubic lice issue!"

"What the hell?" He grunted.

"You're disgusting!" The redhead told him as she backed away.

"Cheryl," he protested, "I've never seen this woman before in my life." But she was gone before he could finish his sentence.

He turned to me angrily. "What the hell are you playing at? You demented witch."

"I've met men like you before," I told him sternly. "Men who think that a woman is only worth what they can give you. Men who think that we're all here for your pleasure."

"You know nothing about me." He argued.

"Maybe not," I agreed, "but I think I've got your measure." I thought of Helen.

I thought of the men who would come to the house and stick around for as long as they were getting what they wanted before they disappeared. I thought of the men who beat my mother when she refused to toe the line.

"Hayley had a moment of weakness," I told him. "She's going through a difficult time and I think she just wanted to feel like she had won somehow, but having anything to do with you would have made her a loser."

"I get it," he laughed cockily. "You're her little bitch. You want to play scissor sisters and I'm just getting in the way." I wondered if this man could be any more repulsive.

"Do you know what Alan?" I shook my head. "I don't think you will ever get it. I don't think you're capable of getting it. You're far too closely linked to the Neanderthal to understand anything other than grunts." I shook my head again. "I'll spell it out for you. When you talk to a woman keep your hands to yourself and your eyes on her face. When you try to take advantage of the weak and the vulnerable it says far more about you than it does about them. When you see someone in pain, don't see it as an opportunity to take advantage of the situation."

I turned and walked away. Angrily, deliberately and very quietly. As I started to walk, I heard a pair of hands starting to clap, followed by another, then another. Soon over half the people in the bar were clapping. A smug smile played with my lips yet tears stung my eyes. A lump formed in my throat and my heart thumped in my chest, reminding me I was very much alive.

When I returned to the room, Haley was looking radiant in a flowing deep blue dress. Her blonde hair was pinned up in an off centred bun. Her big blue eyes were even more exaggerated with dark eyeliner and eye shadow. More than a little embarrassed, I didn't recall the events in the bar to Hayley.

"Did you talk to him?" Hayley asked.

"I couldn't find him." I lied. "I asked the bartender and he said he had left with a redhead, I don't think you need to worry."

"Thank you." She smiled.

"Anytime." I smiled back.

At dinner, we ordered another bottle of champagne. The effects of the earlier bottle had worn off so I didn't feel too worried.

"We're going to play a game," Hayley announced.

"Really?" I raised my eyebrows. "Are we fifteen now?"

"Play ball Hope."

"We'll see, what is the game?"

"Right." She answered gleefully. "It's called I have never." I knew the game, but I let her continue. "So, I will say 'I have never.....' then I'll say something I have never done. If you have done it then you take a drink, or you have to tell the story."

"Sounds messy," I replied.

"It'll be fun." She argued. "I'll start."

I shrugged, "Fine."

"Ok," she replied excitedly as the waiter served my rare steak with mushrooms and steak cut chips and Hayley's salad. "I have never eaten baked beans."

"Never?" I couldn't believe that she had never eaten beans, the staple of the working class.

"Nope, never." She shook her head. "The smell knocks me sick."

"Ok, well clearly I have eaten beans," I replied. "Can't exactly tell you a story about it, nothing much to say." Hayley shrugged and accepted my answer, keen to get on to juicier stuff.

"Your turn." She declared.

"I have never run a red light." My mind started working on my next declaration. I wanted to keep it as light as possible, yet make it funny too. Try to help Hayley to enjoy the evening without giving away too much.

Hayley lifted her glass and took a sip. I raised my eyebrow at her, she shrugged in reply.

"I have never had a threesome."

"Hayley, this is me. Obviously no!" I pulled my face at the ridiculous notion.

"I have never drunk tequila." I decided upon.

"No!" Hayley said in the most exaggerated way. "I have had so many great nights on tequila."

"I'm not really into spirits of any kind," I confessed.

"I have never had a fight," Hayley announced.

I sipped at my drink.

"What's the story behind that one?" She asked.

"No story," I shrugged. "sometimes you have to defend yourself."

I thought of Amy and the bullies throughout my school days. The taunting, pushing and constant name-calling. I thought of the times I was ignored completely. The time when Amy and her friends had decided to pretend they couldn't see me so walked into me and ignored everything I said.

I remembered thc time there had been a school trip to an ice rink. My whole class went on that trip, but Helen couldn't find the money. I stayed in school with a much younger class. I helped them with their maths and their artwork. I enjoyed the day despite myself. I walked home alone at the end of the school day. I got home to find my mother had been shopping. I found the receipts, she had spent hundreds on shoes, bags and mini skirts. That night I cried myself to sleep.

“I have never been ice skating,” I announced.

“Never?” She asked dismayed.

“It was never a priority,” I said sadly.

“There’s a rink in Deeside. I had lessons when I was younger.” Hayley told me. “I was quite good.”

“Maybe we can go some time, you can teach me.”

“Yes, that would be nice.” I smiled.

“I have never done karaoke.” She said.

I smirked and sipped my drink. I thought about Ben and I in our drunken rendition of Creep by Radiohead. I blushed at the thought of our fight when he had kissed me. My reaction now seemed so foolish.

“Ben took me out for my thirtieth birthday and made me sing karaoke.” I nodded my head and smirked as I spoke. I had never told anyone about the night.

“Ben had such a thing for you back then,” Hayley laughed. “everyone could see it apart from you.”

A tear formed in my eye.

Hayley patted my hand gently. “It all worked out in the end.” She spoke quietly.

“Not quite.” I looked her in the eye.

18

I awoke to the sound of the hairdryer. Hayley sat in front of the mirror looking fresh and beautiful. My lips felt dry and cracked. I tried to move in the bed, my head felt as though it was stuck to the pillow.

"Morning." Greeted Hayley with a bright smile plastered on her face. The perpetually grinning Barbie Doll from Toy Story came to mind. I felt guilty at the thought.

"Hmm." I groaned.

"Are you feeling a little delicate?" She asked smugly. I knew from experience that Hayley never seemed to get hungover.

"I'll be ok," I mumbled as I dragged myself out of bed and shuffled to the bathroom. Unable to consider standing for long enough to shower I ran the bath. The tub was huge, using it for the second time during my stay seemed a little indulgent, but I figured that I needed to indulge.

The long soak in the bath seemed to do me good and by breakfast time I had managed to shake off the hangover.

We sat in the restaurant, Hayley nibbled on a bowl of muesli with yoghurt, while I tucked into a plate of sausage, bacon, eggs and mushrooms. Washed down with a pot of tea and a glass of orange juice.

"So today?" I ventured.

"Yes, today," Hayley replied with a huge grin. "We're meeting Becky in about half an hour," she glanced at her watch as she spoke, "she's a personal shopper, does a lot of stuff for the WOD's."

WOD's was the pet name that Hayley had adopted for the wives of David's doctor friends. I smiled at the reference. I was nothing like a

WOD and the idea of me being dressed by one of their shoppers was slightly unnerving. I liked to think I had my own style. I liked the way I dressed. I liked the fact that I wasn't a carbon copy of everyone else. I didn't need false eyelashes and hair extensions to make me feel good about myself. Or maybe that was exactly what I did need. I had never really felt good about myself. I had felt less good about myself since I had lost my baby. A thought popped into my head before I could begin to push it away, 'what makes you think you deserve to feel good about yourself?' And there it was in a nutshell. That was the reason I was unable to move on. Because I was filled with self-loathing. I was filled with a feeling of guilt. I had one job, to protect my unborn baby. I had failed miserably.

"Clearly you're not a WOD." Hayley spoke, snapping me from my thoughts. I raised my eyebrows as I looked at Hayley in a 'What are you trying to say?' expression.

"Most of them dress like they're sixty." she smiled. "Becky is really looking forward to working with you." I nodded sceptically.

We met Becky in a large department store that was known for its high standards and even higher price tags. She was young and pretty. She was tall and slim with thick, long auburn hair. She wore pale blue jeans with designer rips at the knees and a plain white T-shirt that hugged her tiny frame.

"Hi." Becky greeted me with far more enthusiasm than I had anticipated. She held out her hand, a perfect smile fixed to her pretty face. "I'm Becky, we're going to have so much fun shopping today."

I shook her hand politely and returned as warm a smile as I could muster.

"Hi," I spoke warmly. "I'm Hope."

"I'm going to do my own thing for a bit," Hayley announced.

"I thought you were staying." I looked at her open-mouthed.

"I'd only get in the way." She called over her shoulder as she wandered towards the exit.

Becky flashed me another of those smiles, "Let's get started."

She took my measurements, my usual dress size, my shoe size. She then asked me to take a seat, she made me a coffee and disappeared. I sat in the very plush waiting area of the changing room sipping a warm latte and wondering what on earth I was getting in to.

I watched as a young woman struggled to reverse into a changing room with a designer baby buggy. Her arms were laden with items. As she struggled with the door to the fitting room, the collection of clothes tumbled to the floor. She swore under her breath. I jumped up to help her, gathering up the clothes then pushing open the fitting room door.

"Thank-you." She sighed, relieved. I passed her the clothes. I gasped as my eyes were drawn to the baby in the pram. Bright blue eyes stared out from a chubby, round face. The baby was beautiful. I had to fight to hold back the tears. I could imagine holding the baby in my arms. Letting her face rest against my shoulder and sinking my face into her mop of black hair. Part of me wanted to stand there forever, eyes locked with the child, but another part of me wanted to run and hide. Looking at that sweet face was too much of a reminder of what I had lost.

"You're going to love these," Becky called to me, snapping me from my daydream.

"You have a beautiful baby," I told the woman as I handed her the clothes.

"Thank-you." She smiled warmly. She didn't ask the question that I had been asked so many times. The question to which the answer had always been no. I was so thankful that she didn't ask.

Becky pulled a hanging rail full of clothes behind her. I raised my eyebrows at the range of colours that I had never even considered wearing.

"Right then," she announced, "I've got some stuff that I know you'll love, but I've also got some accent pieces from our new range that I know will suit you, but they're perhaps not your usual thing."

'Too right.' I thought to myself as I looked at the rail.

"We'll start with this." She pulled a bright orange dress from the rail.

"I'm not sure," I told her as she passed it to me.

"Try it on, see what you think."

Reluctantly I took the dress. In the changing room, I slipped off my jeans and T-Shirt and slithered into the dress. I stood in front of the mirror and gasped. The skirt was short, even on my five-foot frame it barely covered my butt. I had lost weight in recent weeks, but the dress did nothing to flatter my figure. The strapless top was low cut down to my belly button. My breasts spilling out, my nipples barely covered. The bright almost neon colour exaggerated my pale skin tones. My legs looked pale, exposed and dumpy. I couldn't believe that a so-called professional personal shopper had chosen such an item for me.

I popped my head out of the fitting room, making sure to hide my body behind the door.

"Err," I glared at Becky with wide eyes. "What else have you got?"

"Come on out, let me take a look at it."

"No!" I insisted. "It's definitely not for me."

"We need to talk about what's not right about it so we can find a good match for you." I reluctantly stepped out from the fitting room, tugging at the top, trying desperately to keep my breasts in check and tugging at the skirt to cover my lower half. In all the dress had about as much fabric as one of Jo-Jo's handkerchiefs.

Becky smirked a little, then started to laugh. My eyes widened. I wanted to say 'You picked the fucking thing, don't laugh at me!'

"I always like to start with something totally unsuitable," she spoke softly, "sorry about the shock, you look so uncomfortable in that dress."

"Well, yes I am."

"Ok," She spoke softly, "so many women buy the latest fashion and expect that it's going to look great on them because it looks great on the model. The truth is that it doesn't work that way. You have to find what looks great on you. For you, this colour is totally off. You have pale skin so we don't want something that's going to make you look washed out. You need to go for quite dark colours, but then lighten it up too. Blues and greys, browns. They'll all work for you. If I were you, I'd add colour through the right jewellery or accents. Great shoes or a great bag can work wonders."

"Ok," I spoke hesitantly.

"Try this." Becky passed me another dress. It was a deep bottle green colour that I would never choose. I grabbed the garment, desperate to change out of the orange monstrosity.

The green dress was longer. A loose, flowing skirt brushed my knee. The top was conservative with capped shoulders and a high neckline. I swirled in front of the mirror, wishing I had spent more time on my makeup this morning. I looked at my face in the mirror. My chin seemed too pointy, my nose too long. I had always hated my full lips, even now when people were paying hundreds to have lip fillers, I felt that my lips were too fat. My complexion was mottled and uneven.

Yet. As I swirled in front of the mirror, the green dress hugging my slender waist, my hair swishing as I moved. I didn't feel as ugly as I normally did. Somehow the image before me seemed passable. I stood on tiptoes and tried to imagine my bare feet in dainty heels. I scooped up my hair and piled it on top of my head. I pulled my face at the mirror, unsure. 'Maybe' I thought to myself.

I tried on dress after dress. Each time coming out to the changing area for an appraisal from Becky. The ones that I thought might be passable Becky felt were terrible. The dresses Becky chose were utterly wrong for me. "But I don't want something that will draw attention," I told her time and again. She would pull her face in confusion, but shrug and say, "Let's try this one."

It felt like we had been there for hours when Becky handed me a deep purple dress. The silk fabric shimmered in the light. The skirt was slightly shorter than I would have chosen, but not so short that I wouldn't feel comfortable. The shoulder straps were about an inch wide. The neckline was heart-shaped. The back fastened high but then was open at the back. The dress hugged my figure, accentuating my waist and breasts, yet flattering the rest of me. The deep colour suited my complexion. My long hair brushed against my bare back. I gazed in the mirror in wonder. I had never worn a dress that had made me feel this way. I didn't consider that I may be too old or too ugly or too fat to wear such a dress. I felt that this dress permitted me to draw attention. I didn't have to hide from the gazes of others. A dress like this made me just as beautiful as any of the WODs.

Nervously I stepped out of the fitting room. I was surprised to see that Hayley had returned. She and Becky were chatting. As I opened the door, they stopped dead. Their gaze turned to me. Mouths open they looked at me fixedly.

"Wow." Hayley was the first to speak. "Oh, Hope!"

Becky smiled. "I think that's the one."

I nodded in agreement with a smile on my face.

"Next shoes and jewellery," Becky announced. I was reminded of my favourite Disney film Aladdin. The Genie was in the middle of granting Aladdin's first wish, to make him a prince. He had changed his clothes and turned Abu into an elephant, he then rolled up his sleeves and announced: "we're not done yet."

The rest of the afternoon was dedicated to selecting shoes, handbags and jewellery. I was bored and compliant by the time we got to hair and makeup. I even allowed the makeup artist to accentuate my brows with a pencil. I thought of the conversations that Ben and I had when we had smirked at uneven eyebrows, comparing them to slugs. Ben would offer to draw mine on with a Sharpie. I had never heard of many of the items that the make-up artist had used, let alone bought or used them. Each item was presented along with the sales pitch, from foundation to highlighter, from mascara to setting spray. I smiled politely and nodded at every suggestion, having no intention of buying anything.

When the hair and makeup were finished Becky shepherded me to a fitting room, this one had no mirrors. She passed me the purple dress that had undoubtedly been mine from the moment I tried it on. I slipped into the dress, rolled up the stockings that I had been persuaded to buy. And slipped on the dark purple stiletto shoes.

I stepped out of the fitting room and was greeted with a portable full-length mirror that had been placed there to harvest my reaction. I gaped at my reflection, barely recognising the woman who looked back at me. My long dark hair was full and curled, pinned on one side. Diamante earrings adorned my ears. My delicate neck was highlighted by a diamante choker. My lips were painted a deep red colour. My eyes heavily made up with flicks in the corners, giving them a cat-like quality. The false eyelashes I had been persuaded to wear appeared too big. I felt something like a Barbie doll. Again, Aladdin came to mind. The scene when Aladdin is going to meet the princess. The Genie had been trying to persuade Aladdin to come clean and tell the princess who he really was. Aladdin refused. He turned to the Genie and asked: "How do I look?" The Genie replied, "Like a Prince." Full of disappointment.

I felt beautiful. Every aspect of the makeover seemed to enhance my features. I felt more beautiful than I had ever felt. I also felt like a fraud.

Hayley pulled onto the driveway back at home. I dragged my case from the back seat. I looked at the house with surprise. It was clear that Ben had been busy. The lawns were perfectly manicured, the windows had been cleaned.

The house was in darkness. I was disappointed. For the first time in a long time, I had been looking forward to seeing Ben.

"Thanks for coming with me." I flashed a smile at Hayley. I had genuinely enjoyed her company over the past two days.

"You're welcome." She smiled in return. "I've enjoyed it," she winked, "you little pisshead."

We both laughed.

"You look stunning Hope." She said softly. "You are stunning, you've always been so beautiful." I was shocked by her words.

I had never seen myself as pretty. Whenever I looked in the mirror I saw nothing except my flaws yet in that moment I felt beautiful. I felt refreshed and hopeful for the future. I was ready to let go of my pain, to stop punishing myself for what had happened. I wanted to rebuild my life.

"Thank you," I replied bashfully.

"What are you going to do?" I asked her. We both knew I was referring to David. Neither of us had mentioned him or the affair since the previous afternoon. It had been the proverbial elephant in the room. Both of us thinking about what had been said, but neither of us finding the words.

She shrugged. "I really don't know." Her voice was full of sadness. I wasn't sure if it had always been there and I just hadn't noticed it before.

"You need to talk to him." I ventured softly.

"I know." She nodded, "But not tonight."

I smiled in agreement. I took her hand in mine.

“We’ve been friends for more than twenty years,” I told her with the utmost sincerity. “After this weekend I feel I know you better than I ever have.” I smiled. “Maybe it’s good to let people see your weaknesses from time to time?”

She smiled knowingly. “Oh, I have none of those.” She shirked. “Go knock ‘em dead.” She winked as I walked towards the door.

Her words disarmed me. Knock who dead? What a strange thing to say.

19

There was a hushed silence as I opened the door, a strange and surreal feeling overtook me. I felt as though I was in a dream. I was walking into my home, yet it felt different. I flicked on the light in the hallway. My surroundings were slowly illuminated. The table in the hall with the phone and a porcelain bowl where we threw our keys. The tiled floor was spotlessly clean, even the door handles had been polished, I didn't even know that Ben knew that was a thing. The doors to every room were closed which I found strangely disconcerting. I was sure I could hear shuffling noises coming from the lounge. My heart started beating faster. I felt vulnerable and alone stood in the hallway of my home that didn't quite feel like home. I was afraid of the sounds that I heard. Was there an intruder? I spun around towards the door, ready to run back out and drag Hayley in to help me check for intruders. I was shocked to see her shadow through the glass of the front door.

"Surprise!" a chorus of voices shouted at once.

Suddenly every door had swung open. Party poppers bursting all around me spreading streamers and confetti all over the perfectly polished floor. People appeared from nowhere and filled the hall. Ben was in front of me. His face beaming with joy.

"Wow!" He exclaimed grasping my shoulders. "You look amazing." He kissed me on the mouth before I had the chance to respond.

Suddenly he was gone. I felt Mandy hugging me before I even realised she was there. "Happy Birthday chuck." She said as she planted a kiss on my cheek. I was utterly bewildered, Mandy worked in the purchasing department at Eco build. I had been on leave since the miscarriage. I had not seen or spoken to anyone from work since I had lost the baby. I hadn't decided if I would ever return to the office. I had secretly been planning to slip away and join another architectural firm. I was in total bemusement.

Before I could process my thoughts, Derek, from HR was hugging me. "Hope," he greeted me warmly, "it's so great to see you looking so well after everything." I wanted to throw my arms up in the air and scream 'Stop!'

The wave of well-wishers never seemed to end. Mostly there were people from work, or Ben's friends and family. His mum, who I had refused to see since we lost the baby, his Aunt Aida who was a complete busy body and always had a view on other peoples' lives. There must have been fifty or sixty people at the party. Neighbours, work colleagues, Ben's friends and family. All wishing me well. Some expressing their sorrow for my loss, most awkwardly wishing me happy birthday in an 'I don't really know you, but I like Ben so I'm here anyway' sort of way.

I politely thanked people for coming. I moved through the lounge to the dining room, through the kitchen to the large conservatory that Ben and I had built a year earlier. Every room was filled with well-wishers and party-goers. I graciously accepted a glass of wine that was handed to me, but I didn't take a sip. Music started to blare from the stereo. An eclectic mix of rock, indie, folk and pop music that could only have been collated with me in mind. The house was gleaming. In the dining room, there was an extensive buffet that Ben had ordered in. Above the table was a banner saying "Happy 40th Birthday Hope". There was a photo album on the coffee table in the lounge. The front cover read "Happy 40th Birthday Hope." I opened the book to be greeted with an image of my eighteen-year-old self. Heavily mascaraed, with black lips and jet black hair. My face set in a scowl. Under the photo was a caption reading 'You've always had your own sense of style, but that's what I love about you.' On the next page was an image of me sat at my drawing board in the office at work. A pencil tucked behind my ear and a look of pure concentration on my face. Seeing the photograph brought back the day it had been taken so clearly in my mind.

I was twenty-seven. I had been working at the office since I had qualified. Ben was new to the office, he was in charge of IT and had been working on a website to promote the architectural firm. He had taken lots of photographs of everyone, but I had refused to take part. The one he had taken of me had been late at night. I was always the last one to leave the office. There never seemed to be anything to go home for and I was always so immersed in my work. My life at that time was lonely. I wouldn't have admitted that to anyone then, or even now. I wanted to fit in but never did. I always said the wrong thing or rubbed people up the wrong way.

The office had been in darkness except for a desk lamp that illuminated my drawing board. I was utterly absorbed in what I was doing, so much so that I didn't notice Ben stood at the other end of the office. It was only when I heard the shutter and saw the flash of light from the camera that I looked up. I saw the shadowy figure at the other end of the office and immediately recognised the cute new guy. Suddenly I was nervous, anxious. "Ben?" I asked.

"I knew I'd get one of you." He grinned.

"Ben that's not fair." I protested. I had told him repeatedly that I didn't want to be on the website.

"You need to be part of it." He told me sincerely. "You're an important part of the business."

I blushed. I always blushed around him.

My attention was drawn to the caption under the photograph. "I admired you from the moment we met." I blushed at the thought. The album was full of photographs. Page after page of images, mainly of me trying to dodge the camera. Each photograph had an equally cheesy caption. I felt sick. I placed the album on the shelf under the table and wandered into the hall. The kitchen door was open. Ben was surrounded by party guests. He was recounting some tale or another. The guests were attentive, hanging on his every word. I was able to slip away unnoticed.

The partygoers had done their duty and wished me well, now I could go back to being nothing. As I reached the top of the stairs I heard a burst of loud laughter. Ben had reached the climax of his story. I slipped into the bedroom and collapsed on the bed in a heap of tears.

20

When I first started to drive my thoughts were muddied by a thick fog. I had no plan, no design to my journey. I simply needed to drive. Two hours had passed when the mist of my mind started to fade away and I told myself where I was heading. As I realised where my heart was taking me, I almost stopped in stunned silence. Was it the right thing to do? Could I face it after all of the years that had passed? But I knew those questions were futile. I had begun the journey. I had taken this journey a thousand times in my dreams. Now it was time to take the journey in reality.

I drove for four hours straight. I had heard my phone buzzing with notification after notification but I had ignored everyone. By three in the morning, I was exhausted. Road signs reminded me that tiredness can kill. Both physically and emotionally exhausted I pulled into a service station and parked up my car. I reached for my phone and opened Whatsapp. There were ten notifications from Ben and Six from Hayley.

I replied.

3:15 am - "I'm safe. Sounds like you enjoyed your party. I need to take a break from things. Give me some time. I'll call you when I'm ready."

With that, I switched off my phone, grabbed the small bag I had packed hastily and headed into the service station in the desperate search of a toilet. I elicited a range of confused looks as I followed the signs to the ladies.

As I was washing my hands, I looked in the mirror. The heavy makeup on my eyes had smudged, despite the fixing spray. My curls were tousled and the clip holding my hair to one side had slipped.

I took a makeup wipe from my bag and removed as much of the makeup as I could. I pulled at the false eyelashes until they sprang free. I dropped them into the sink and there they sat like two demented millipedes. I removed the earrings and the choker and slipped them into my clutch bag.

I returned to the stall and changed into jeans and a T-Shirt. I glanced into the mirror once more before I left. 'Once a street rat, always a street rat.' slipped into my thoughts.

Before leaving the service station I withdrew £500 in cash from my bank account. As I tucked the money into my purse I saw the card for the joint account. I shrugged to myself, 'why not?' I thought, withdrawing a further £500 from the joint account. I tried to tell myself that I wasn't being deliberately evasive, but I knew that wasn't true. The fact was that I knew how to disappear. Step one was to only deal with cash.

I stretched as I pulled to a stop in the car park of The Meadows guest house. I was still stiff from my sleep in the service station car park. A night with a gear stick rammed into your thigh is hardly refreshing. I was nervous about my return to Port Merdow. I considered turning the car around and driving away, but then an image of my imaginary friend slipped into my mind. Her lips parted and I heard my voice as she said: "You know how to find the truth."

I knew that it was now or never. Despite my fears, I stepped out of the car and threw my bags over my shoulder. I forced myself to hold my head high as I walked purposefully up the steps to the Hotel reception.

Billy Mayer was working on reception. I recognised him almost instantly from my primary school. His crooked smile and cocky manner had barely changed, but his hair had now all but disappeared. His once very slender figure had become somewhat rotund. I nervously smoothed my hair. I felt a little flustered. I wondered how I might be judged, although why I should care was beyond me.

"Hi," I plonked my bag down as I approached the counter. "I'd like a single room please."

Billy flashed me a smile, his crooked teeth on full display. "Of course." He grinned. "And what brings you to Port Merdow?" Was he flirting with me? I couldn't quite tell.

"Uh, oh, just visiting," I mumbled. He didn't recognise me, for which I was thankful.

"Well, I can recommend our beautiful beach, although I'm not sure it's quite bikini weather." As he winked, I'm fairly sure that the distaste I felt showed on my face.

"Thank you." I smiled politely as I reached for the room key that he had placed on the counter. Hastily I paid cash for the room for three nights. I wasn't sure if that would be enough time, but it was a start.

The events of the weekend were still playing with my mind when I drifted off to sleep. My dreams were plagued with incoherent images. In my dream, I was on the extreme makeover show. The host was about to reveal the results of my makeover. I had been subjected to a catalogue of surgeries and treatments. I had been made to look taller and slimmer. I'd had significant plastic surgery. My hair and makeup had been perfected and I had been dressed by a specialist stylist. In my dream, everyone was waiting for the revelation. Ben's family and friends were stood waiting along with colleagues from work. Hayley was stood with David, holding his hand tenderly. On David's other side stood a tall, slim woman who looked like a younger version of Hayley. The younger woman held David's other hand, her head rested on his shoulder.

I walked down the steps, nervously looking out at those waiting to see my transformation. I was greeted by a chorus of gasps and 'ohs'. At the bottom of the stairs was a mirror shrouded with a curtain.

"Are you ready to see the new you?" The host asked me, excited anticipation in his voice. I nodded hesitantly. The host whipped away the curtain in one swish movement. I stood and stared at the image in front of me, mouth open in shock and awe. The image looking back at me wasn't me at all. It was Hayley.

I awoke with a start. Sweat dripping down my forehead. I glanced at my phone. I checked the time, ignoring the flashing notifications for WhatsApp and Messenger. It was five pm. I had slept for hours. I decided it was time to head out.

The village where I grew up was the kind of place you found in picture postcards. It was neatly tucked away along the South West coast with imposing cliff tops and a soft, sandy beach. In the summer the local guest houses would be filled with tourists who would flood the beach, cafés and restaurants. Often complaints could be heard about how there was little to do in the town and that it was a prime location begging for a developer to come in and exploit the landscape. I loved my village as it was. It was not in need of development or investment or any more tourists for that matter. It was the sort of town that people never left. Everyone knew each other and everyone knew each other's business. The sense of community could feel like a warm embrace for most, but for those who were different, those who didn't quite fit in, Port Merdow could be desolate and isolating.

I had not seen the village in over twenty years, yet I knew every stone of the cobbled streets. As I wandered through the village drinking in the sights and sounds I felt the warmth of its familiarity. The main street had become a little more developed. Some of the houses had now become shops and restaurants. There was a new Italian restaurant called Mario's.

The butchers, the bakers and the local grocers had all become tourist shops, selling postcards, beach towels, buckets and spades and imported souvenirs.

I had noticed a supermarket on the outskirts of the village on my way in. The post office had been transformed into an arcade with flashing lights and beeping machines calling for people to unload their money into them for the chance of winning an imported piece of plastic something or another. Along the beachfront were an array of bars and a café that had not been there when I had last been to the town. I smiled when I saw the sign for The Catchers Keep in its usual spot. I would visit another day.

I stopped at a bar called the Dolphin and ordered a vodka and coke. I sipped the toxic liquid as I gazed out across the beach. The view was beautiful and imposing. The sun was low in the sky but had not yet begun its final descent into the sea. The sand was soft and inviting, I could imagine the familiar sensation of the warm sand sifting through my toes. On the right-hand side of the bay was a small harbour with a few tiny fishing boats lay moored on the sand. A string of buoys tethered together marked the path for fishing boats. A few sandcastles remained on the beach, but soon the tide would come home and wash them away to create a fresh canvas for the next day's visitors. To the left, the cliffs stood imposingly with the jagged rocks at their feet. Steps had been carved into the rocks to allow people to reach the beach from the top. Tall dune grass grew from every available crevice. Life taking hold wherever it could. The cliff tops were rich with grasses and wildflowers, their sweet perfume was drifting down and filling my lungs. I could just see the rooftop of Treth Chy, the house where I grew up. The familiar red roof tiles glimmering in the evening sun. I closed my eyes and I became my six-year-old self.

21

I woke up early. I could hear the television blaring in the living room. The sun had found its way through the crack in my curtain and I watched as the specs of dust floated in the rays of light. Sleepily I climbed out of bed. My feet padded along the cold tiled floor as I followed the sound of the TV. I stopped abruptly as I walked into the living room. My mother Helen lay on the sofa. The smell of sweat and stale vodka hung in the air and made me feel ill. Yet again she had slept in front of the TV in her clothes. Mascara was smudged under her eyes, her hair was a tangled mess. Drool was dripping from the corner of her mouth. I scanned the room, to make sure nobody else was here. Fear overtook my body. I needed to escape. Escape the smell, the sight, the fear I felt when I looked at her. I ran to my room and quickly slipped on the shorts and T-Shirt I had worn the day before. I pulled my hair into an untidy ponytail and quietly I crept out of the back door. I picked up my shiny red bucket and headed towards the beach. Slowly and quietly I crept at first, but then I started to run. Faster and faster my bare feet pounded across the flower-filled meadow on the cliff top, toward the steps. I ran down the steps, taking care not to slip on the hard, cold rock. When I reached the beach below it felt like a victory. An escape. Freedom from the oppression of the house. I turned towards the rocks. Delighted at the sights as my tiny feet sloshed in the water. Fish darting away from me as I jumped into the pools.

Excitement washed over me as I saw a bright orange crab. It was small. Just big enough to fit into my tiny hand. Determinedly I grabbed the tiny creature from the pool and plunged it into my bucket. I grinned widely. Proud of my find. I wanted to share my prize. For a split second the name Faith crossed my mind, but that was just silly. I was too old for imaginary friends. I was a big girl.

"Jo-Jo," I thought with a smile.

When I reached the top of the cliff I looked right towards my own home, then turned my head towards Jo-Jo's pretty pink cottage. Baskets of flowers filled the veranda and the smell was always sweet and welcoming. The water in my bucket sloshed as I climbed the steps to her front door. Nervously I thought I was going to lose my find.

"Jo-Jo" I shouted excitedly as I knocked at the door. I jumped from one foot to another giddy to show Jo-Jo what I had found. "Well, hello young lady." Her warm voice was like a hug. I grinned, eager to please her. I held the bucket behind my back. The water sloshing as I rocked from side to side.

"Look what I found!" I grinned as I presented her with the bucket.

"Wow!" She smiled warmly. "Where did you find that?" her voice was calm, but suddenly I felt worried. I might get into trouble. I wasn't supposed to go down to the beach. Not on my own. It was dangerous. Helen had told me I wasn't allowed. Now with Jo-Jo looking at me, I was frightened that she would stop loving me, that she would stop being kind to me. I was supposed to be good. I was supposed to do what I was told, or no one would want me. My blue eyes started to fill with tears and nervously I backed away.

"Shall we see what sort of crab you found?" Jo-Jo calmly guided me into her house. "I'm sure I have a book around here somewhere. It has lots of different sea creatures in it. She sat me down on the sofa and went to find the book. When she returned she had orange juice and toast along with a big book about sea creatures. Together we turned the pages looking for my orange crab as I sipped the juice and nibbled the toast.

"He's a very nice crab." Jo-Jo smiled at me. "I think he might prefer to be back home though." I pouted at Jo-Jo. I didn't want him to go back. I wanted him to be mine. "did you get him from the rock pools?" Jo-Jo enquired calmly. I reluctantly nodded, waiting to be scolded or slapped, or worse. "Did you go down there with Helen?" I shook my head, tears starting to fill my eyes again. "It's ok." She told me, "you're not in

trouble, but you know that it's dangerous down there. If the tide were to come in, or if someone were to take you, there wouldn't be a lot you could do."

"I didn't like the smell." Fat tears rolled down my cheeks now.

"The smell?" Jo-Jo looked puzzled. "The smell of the sea?"

I shook my head, "Helen." I pulled a face. "She always smells that way, but today it was worst. She was asleep and she didn't wake up she looked scary."

Jo-Jo nodded knowingly. "You know your mummy loves you don't you?" I shrugged. It seemed such a nothing thing to say. I didn't think that Helen loved me. She never did. She loved to get drunk, to talk to men. She loved to do what she wanted to do. I was always in the way. I was the thing that stopped her from being happy. I always saw it when she looked at me.

"She does love you. More than you will ever know." I looked at the floor, I didn't know where else to look. "The trouble is that your mummy is very sad and very hurt. She doesn't know how to love herself." I didn't understand what Jo-Jo meant, but those words have always stayed with me. "One day you might understand. The only thing we can do now is to be good for Helen." Jo-Jo smiled and took my hand. "be good for your Mummy." I looked into her big brown eyes. Her eyes searched mine for understanding or agreement, or both. She crouched down so she was eye to eye with me. "You know you shouldn't have gone down to the beach alone don't you Hope?" A tear sprung into the corner of my eye and I nodded slowly and sullenly. "You mustn't go out of the house without your Mummy, not unless the place is on fire, you understand that don't you?" I nodded again. I wanted to say I was sorry, but I knew the words wouldn't come out through my sorrow. "Shall I take you home?" I knew it wasn't really a question, but Jo-Jo wanted me to feel I had some control of the situation. She raised from her crouched position and started to lead me gently towards the door. As we reached the telephone table in the hall she stopped. Almost as an afterthought, she asked, "You know my phone number don't you Hope?" I nodded.

"If ever you're afraid, or sad or if you're alone," a look that I didn't quite understand crossed her face, "you call my number." She smiled, but it didn't seem like her normal warm and happy smile, this smile was covering something else, fear maybe? "I'll come over and help your Mummy when you need me to."

"Ok." I squeaked.

"Maybe we don't even have to tell her that you called? I'll just pop over to borrow some milk or to have a cup of tea." I smiled at this. I liked the idea that Jo-Jo would come over when I asked her to. I liked it when Jo-Jo visited. Helen was kinder and happier when Jo-Jo was around.

22

"Is this seat taken?" A voice woke me from my thoughts. I looked up, bewildered and saw a man stood looking at me. His eyes were the brightest of blue, his dark hair was cut short at the sides, the top was long, almost in a quiff.

"Err, no," I answered in bemused surprise. I wanted to point out that there were several empty tables, but I somehow stopped myself from being so rude.

He sat down. A cheeky smile on his face and a twinkle in his blue eyes.

"I'm Jon," His voice was soft with a whisper of a faded Irish accent. His chiselled face broke into a broad smile. White teeth lined up to greet me, the twinkle in his eye promised laughter and fun and everything that my heart had yearned for so very long.

I returned the smile and held out my hand, I was about to introduce myself then decided to air on the side of caution. So far, I had not been recognised in the small town, but that wasn't to say that would continue. Hope was a fairly unusual name, "Emily." I replied softly.

"Well Emily," he flashed that smile again, "It's an absolute pleasure to meet you."

I nodded with a smile.

"What are you drinking?" I looked at the remnants of my drink.

"Vodka and coke," I replied, "but I'm just about to head off."

"Sit a while," he smiled "have a drink with me."

I knew that he was far too charming and far too flirty for this to be anything but a well-rehearsed routine, I also knew that I had a husband and I had no right flirting with strange men. I tried to convince myself that chatting to him would be perfectly innocent. Deep down I knew that what he wanted was far from innocent. Men like him had no intention of innocent conversations that led nowhere. If I accepted his offer of a drink it would no doubt give him the impression that he was due something in return. I thought of Helen. Of the black eyes and burst lips that had been a far too regular feature of her pretty face. I thought of the times I would hear shouting as I buried my head under my pillow.

"No, thank-you." I smiled politely. "I really only stopped to drink it all in." I motioned to the view.

"It is a lovely view." He gazed out towards the sea. By now the sun had all but disappeared beneath the waves, casting bright reds and oranges over the horizon. Lamps were illuminating the seafront. The tide was coming in like a soft blanket covering the sand.

The air was starting to feel slightly chilly and I pulled my leather jacket on. I picked up my glass and drank down the last of the liquid. I picked up my handbag and rested it on my shoulder as I stood.

"Won't ya have one more drink with me?" he grabbed my wrist, trying to make me sit down once more.

"Thank you," I replied sternly, "but not tonight. There's somewhere I need to be."

"C'mon Emily." He tried to sound charming, but there was a seedy undertone to his voice that made me feel uncomfortable.

"Let go of my arm please." I dropped any pretence of friendliness. I looked at him sternly. "I don't quite know what you expect to achieve by acting like a prick, but go and try it on with someone who might welcome your Neanderthal approach."

"Who the feck do you think yer talking to?" He practically grunted the words. I was starting to feel nervous. I scanned the vicinity looking for someone who might intervene.

"Just let go of my arm," I softened my tone, trying to appear charming, "go back inside, find your mates and have a great night."

"How about we go back to your room and you and me can have a great night?" His words made me feel sick.

"That's never going to happen," I spoke confidently, despite my heart pounding in my chest. His grip on my arm had tightened and it was starting to hurt. I was terrified of what he might do but knew better than to show it.

"Why are you being such a cock tease?" He growled.

"Tell me," I spoke angrily this time, "when has this approach ever actually got you what you're looking for?" I yanked at my arm hoping to break free. I shook my head in disbelief, "You're a good-looking bloke. You don't need to act like a prick. You were so charming when you first came over to speak to me. Just because I'm not interested doesn't mean that you have to regress to being a caveman." His grip loosened as I spoke. "I'm sure you have plenty of girls who are interested in you, but my advice is to find a decent one and treat her right."

"You're just loving being a tease, though aren't ya?" He grumbled.

"I'm not being a tease. I just don't want to have a drink, or go to my hotel with anyone, none of that." I sighed as I spoke, "I tell you one thing for sure though, if I had been up for any of that then your attitude would have soon changed my mind."

"What's going on?" I was relieved to hear a voice behind me. As I turned to see where the voice had come from Jon let go of my arm. I recognised the stranger walking towards me. I wondered if he recognised me.

"Ah, we're just chattin'," Jon answered. I raised my eyebrows, but he didn't seem to notice.

"Why don't you leave the lady alone mate?" He spoke in a voice I hadn't heard for over twenty years but recognised instantly. Kevin had shown me kindness when I had needed it and for that, I would always be grateful.

Kevin looked a little bewildered as he came closer. "Hope?" he asked, his head tilted to one side. I nodded. A warm smile spread across his face. Before I could react, his arms were wrapped around me in a warm embrace. I felt so comforted in his arms, so safe and secure. I hadn't meant to cry, but I seemed unable to stop myself.

He sat me down at the table and sat in the seat next to me. His face full of concern. I looked up as Jon disappeared back into the bar.

In essentials, Kevin hadn't changed at all, but time hadn't been too kind to him. His hair was still thick and full, but it was now spattered with white. Time had left its marks on his face. He had lost the sparkle and joy from his eyes.

"Where have you been? What happened? You just disappeared." There were too many questions at once and I struggled to process my thoughts and emotions.

I sighed. "I err." I took a deep breath as I gathered my thoughts. I struggled to hold back the tears. "I live in Chester."

He nodded. "But where did you go?"

"I started at University in Sheffield." I had seen my life in two parts. Part one had been my childhood in Port Merdow and everything that entailed, part two had begun when I went to University. I had started a new life and left the old one behind. I had been careful to separate the two, but here was Kevin wanting to know about part two. He was firmly in part one and I felt uncomfortable allowing him to slip into the former, but isn't that what I had done by returning? I knew I had to stop hiding from the past.

"I went through the clearing system," I revealed. "I wanted a fresh start. I wanted to go somewhere that nobody knew me."

He nodded, understanding my motives.

"I studied Architecture." I omitted the fact that I had finished top of my class with a first.

"You're an architect?" I nodded yes. "Wow!"

"Yeah," I said. "I work for a company in Chester that specialises in passive houses."

I smiled bashfully. I always played down my achievement, but my time at university had been incredibly difficult. I had taken a job in a local bar and worked hours on end to help me pay my way.

While the other students were partying, I would either be working on projects or working in the bar. I had been utterly focussed on my goal and nothing was going to stand in my way. If I dropped marks on a project I would pour over my feedback, determined not to make the same mistake again.

I became obsessed with sustainable design, years before it became fashionable.

After graduation, it was vital for me to work with people who shared my values and vision. I found Eco Build in Chester, they were a firm who specialised in buildings with small carbon footprints. I researched the company. Found out every little bit of information that I could about them. I created the perfect cover letter and submitted it along with my CV. I became obsessed. I needed to land that job.

"So, are you married?" Kevin broke my thoughts.

"Yes," I replied. I thought of Ben. I could almost feel his hand wrapped in mine. I thought of the way I felt when we sat together with a glass of wine and a home-cooked meal at the end of the day. The way we would laugh, talk about politics, come up with the same corny jokes. I loved just curling up together watching a film. His arms wrapped around me, protecting me. I smiled.

"His name is Ben."

"Have you been married long?" He asked me. I shook my head.

"Four years." I thought of all the time that Ben and I had lost. The time that we should have shared, but didn't. I thought of the invitations to nights out that I had turned down. I thought of the days when Ben had brought me lunch and coffee because I had been too wrapped up in my work to leave my desk. At the time it had all seemed so important. To me, I was saving the world. I had just forgotten to save myself.

"Are you married?" I asked. Kevin nodded.

"Do you remember Amy?" He asked.

I raised my eyebrows, but I was hardly surprised. Amy had always had a thing for Kevin, ever since junior school. She was pretty and popular, the type of girl who would always get the guy she wanted.

"I used to work for her Dad Mike, at Catchers Keep," I told him.

"He still has that place, down by the harbour"

"Really?" I smiled fondly thinking of Mike. He was so good to me when I worked for him. He knew I wasn't eating well at home so would always make sure I had something to eat before I left. He would give me as many shifts as he thought I could handle because he knew I needed the money, but he would constantly check to make sure it wasn't getting in the way of my studies. "I'll have to pop over there and see him while I'm here."

Kevin laughed. "He could probably retire. In the summer this place gets flooded with tourists and not just idiots like the guy you met. Mike's cafe is always full. Everyone loves the place. He's had offers from big developers wanting to buy it, but be refuses to sell up. Says that he doesn't trust anyone to get it right." I smiled at the thought, it sounded like Mike. "I think he loves it too much, it's like his baby."

"Probably." I agreed laughing. "I remember when I used to work for him, he was obsessed. If a customer failed to clear their entire plate then he would be frantic, worrying about what was wrong."

"He's still the same." Kevin laughed.

I smiled fondly thinking of Mike. He was like the dad I never had.

"Do you have any kids?" Kevin's question hit me like a low blow.

Of course, he had no way of knowing that his question held such deep scars, but he had no way of knowing it didn't.

My stock answer almost slipped out before could think. The answer I had given to people for years. The only answer to that question that gave me hope and optimism. But I didn't reply as I had a thousand times. I didn't say 'not yet.' In the past when I had given that answer I had felt certain that children were very much a part of the plan. I felt that it would happen one day.

"No," I replied quietly. In light of my age, not to mention my current state of mind and the state of my relationship it was becoming very clear to me that the chances were that I would never be a mother. The pain of that thought was like a knife stabbing through my heart. I felt panicked by the idea that I might never have the child I dreamed of. I didn't have the strength to deal with that thought at this moment. I pushed at the thought, desperate to consign it to the furthest reaches of my mind.

"Do you and Amy have kids?" I tried to divert attention from me once more.

Kevin nodded. "Two," he replied with a smile. "The eldest, Mikey is twenty-one." I did some quick maths and tried hard to refrain from raising my eyebrows. "He works on the boats, Amy wanted him to go to Uni, but it was never going to be his thing." I nodded. I was bemused by the thought of someone my age with an adult child. "Kisha is twelve."

He continued. "She is in year seven at the high school." He laughed fondly. "She is the exact opposite of her brother. She is such a little swot. Top of her class in everything." I smiled.

Neither Amy or Kevin had been exceptional students. For them, high school had been a social occasion. Kevin had been captain of the rugby team. He was popular amongst the students and the teachers alike. Amy was pretty with long blonde hair. She looked almost identical to every other girl in the school. She was the type of girl who was terrified to be different as she knew she would be singled out. She was popular for as long as she conformed. She was the type of girl who was friendly when we were alone together, but if she was with her gang of friends, she would resort to put-downs in order to make sure that I became the target of their bullying rather than her. Looking back, I understood how she felt at that time, but being on the receiving end of her hit and miss friendship was difficult.

"And what do you do for a living?" I asked.

"I run this place." He pointed towards the bar. "Most of the jobs around here are either linked to fishing or tourism."

I nodded.

"The guy you were talking to….." Kevin started.

"He was an arse hole," I told him before he could continue.

"Sounds about right," Kevin told me. "He's been in here every night this past week. Him and a group of five or six guys. I think they wanted more of a Magaluf experience."

I laughed at the idea. The town had become more commercialised since I was last here, but it was the type of place that attracted couples, families and the over sixties. "Last night he tried it on with these two girls. It was hilarious to watch because you could tell he was hedging his bets. He would have been happy to take either home."

"He didn't want to take no for an answer," I told Kevin glumly. "He must have had too many knock backs already." I shook my head. "I just don't get blokes like that at all. He was good looking, he was quite charming at first. If only he knew how to behave around women, I am sure he wouldn't be getting so many rejections."

Kevin nodded, but I got the feeling he didn't understand. There were some things that only another women would really understand.

"So, what brings you home?" Kevin asked the question that I had hoped he wouldn't. The question that I didn't really know the answer to.

I shrugged. "Curiosity." I offered.

"Is your husband back at the hotel?" Kevin asked.

I shook my head. "I'm here alone." He tried to hide his knowing expression, but I saw it as he pushed it away with a broad smile.

"Well, we'll have to have drinks or something, on my night off." I nodded. Kevin pulled an order pad from his top pocket. He wrote down his number and passed it to me. "It would be good to catch up properly when I have more time." He glanced back towards the bar, seemingly wondering what sort of mayhem Jon and his gang had caused in his absence.

"Thanks for saving me." I smiled. "You're making a habit of this, that's the second time in just over twenty years."

He smiled and warmly patted me on the arm as he turned away.

"Make sure you call me." I nodded.

I stood and followed the road that ran alongside the beach. Colourful bunting had been hung from the lampposts that lined the road. I watched as a young couple walked hand in hand towards the sea. Their figures silhouetted against the blushing night sky. As they kissed I turned away, feeling as though I was intruding on their moment.

I was reminded of the last time I had seen Kevin. A putrid soup of conflicting emotions threatened to take a hold of me. I closed my eyes. The cool breeze flowed around me. I smelled the sweet salt of the sea air. I was taken back to that August day when I was just eighteen.

~

It was a Saturday in mid-August. I'd been in work at Catchers Keep since early that morning. There had barely been a moment when the tables weren't full all day. Amy's friend Emma was working with us but was pretty hopeless and I had to work extra hard to pick up her slack.

I took out dishes to customers and cleared tables on the way back. I was making three coffees for everyone that she made, all the while taking care to make customers feel welcome.

It was almost five by the time the place started to calm down. I was stood taking an order from a family who were visiting the town for the first time. They had told me how beautiful the place was, how they had been to the beach, how disappointed they were that there wasn't that much to do. I smiled politely and told them that there was a lovely park just outside of town. I told them about Henry Hodgkin's farm where he had a little petting area with rabbits and goats. You could feed the chickens. They smiled politely, but I got the impression they wanted more excitement.

I heard Amy and her friends approaching before I saw them. Uneasily I awaited the taunting and the sideward glances.

I took my customers order, taking care to write everything down correctly then I slipped off to the kitchen hoping that Amy and Co would saunter right by without stopping.

Amy had a habit of dropping by the cafe on Saturday afternoons. She and her friends would order ice-cream, milkshakes and lattes, but do their best to cause mayhem and laugh at me at every opportunity. They always made me feel uneasy.

As I walked out of the kitchen, I heard Emma in a loud voice. "Hey, Aims!" She shouted gleefully. "So great to see a friendly face."

"Emma, hey you," Amy shouted in return. "Has the old guy been working you too hard all day?"

"Oh, my god yes!" Emma exclaimed. "I have not stopped."

I avoided being drawn in as I went to clear a table of dishes that Emma had ignored.

"You sit down with us," Amy instructed, "you poor thing! Hope can take our order. I'm sure Dad won't mind you finishing a little early."

"Amy is here." I worked hard to keep my tone cheerful as I went into the kitchen with the dishes. Mike looked up from where he was preparing the order I had just taken to him. "I heard." He nodded. "I'll go and say hello once I've finished this, ask Emma to pop through to the kitchen." I looked at him with pleading eyes, I didn't want to disobey Amy and her orders. But Mike was the one I worked for.

"It'll be fine." He told me.

I smiled in as friendly a way as I could at Emma as I went out to take the group's order, "Mike said could you just pop back into the kitchen." Again, my voice was bright and breezy. Emma stood up moodily and wandered towards the kitchen. I stood in front of Amy's table. She was with a different crowd this week. I recognised everyone in the group of four but had spoken less than two words to most other than Amy in all of the time I had been at high school.

"What can I get for you?" I asked politely. Telling myself they were just regular customers. Willing myself not to become flustered.

An indecipherable flurry of requests came my way all at once.

"I'll start with you." I turned to Claire and smiled. Claire was the unspoken leader of the group. Confident and self-assured. She never failed to make me feel uneasy. I was determined that today I would stand my ground. Carefully and deliberately I noted down each of the orders. Smiling when I should and being calm and polite until I turned to Kevin.

I knew who Kevin was. Everyone knew who Kevin was. I had never spoken to him since primary school. He wasn't in any of my classes in high school, he had taken sports and music instead of art and design technology so our paths rarely crossed.

"What can I get for you?" I asked politely.

"You're Hope Tegan." Kevin smiled. I noticed the puzzled look on Amy's face.

I nodded. "Yes, I am." I smiled in my 'welcome to Catchers Keep' smile. "What can I get you?"

"You live in that little cottage set back from the clifftop, overlooking the beach." He continued. I wanted to ask 'What is this? This is your life?' but I refrained. I smiled and nodded once more.

"Would you like a milkshake?" I asked.

"I didn't know you worked here." He smiled again. "Have you been here long?"

"Two years," I told him. "I started here just after I finished my GCSE's. Hoping to save a little money to help me through Uni." I ignored the sniggers from Amy. She had no ambition to go to university. Of course, to her the idea of me of all people having ambition was ludicrous. My reputation went before me, or least my mother's did. Kevin smiled and nodded.

"That's really good." He didn't sound patronising and he wasn't ridiculing my dream. He seemed genuinely impressed. "Which Uni are you going to?"

"Edinburgh." I lied. I had not shared my true plans with anyone else.

"The results were out this Thursday weren't they?" Kevin asked. "What did you get?"

I blushed and looked at the floor bashfully. "Three A's and a B," I told him. "I only got a B in Physics, but it was really difficult."

"They're amazing results." He smiled broadly again. Damn that smile was alluring. My pulse was racing.

"Thank you." I smiled at him. There was far too much smiling going on. I could sense that Amy was starting to get jealous of the attention that Kevin was paying to me.

"Anyway." I tried to divert his attention away from me. I was desperate to avoid upsetting Amy. "What would you like to order?"

"Those shakes sound good." He picked up a menu and started to scan through it. "How about blueberry?" I nodded and jotted down his order on my pad.

"I'll be right back." I smiled again as I turned away to make the drinks. Emma had appeared at the counter.

"Mike says I have to help you." She mumbled sulkily.

"Thank you," I replied with forced cheerfulness. "If you do those two coffees, I'll do the shakes."

When I returned to the table with the drinks there was a distinctive, uncomfortable atmosphere. Amy was whispering to Kevin under her breath. Kevin was giving a look that told her to leave it.

"That looks amazing," Kevin commented as I handed him the drink. "Thank you."

"Enjoy," I said as I handed out the rest of the drinks.

"Listen Hope." Kevin flinched as he spoke. Amy had kicked him under the table. "We're all heading to the beach in a while. Claire and Andy got their results on Thursday too, nothing like your results, but they see it as a cause for celebration." Andy laughed along.

"I'm glad to hear you got the results you wanted." I smiled at Claire. She had been in my art class. I envied her artwork, it was utterly amazing. Where my work was far more technical, she had an natural creativity that I craved. "I hope you have a good night."

"Why don't you come too?" Kevin asked. I was shocked and thrilled by the question. Nobody ever invited me anywhere, least of all the most popular kids in the school.

"Oh, I have to go straight home after work." I instinctively told him. Terrified at the thought of imposing upon Amy and her group. "But thank you."

"Come on," Claire spoke this time, again taking me by complete surprise. "It'll be fun. You worked so hard for your A-Levels. You really do deserve a little time to unwind."

"Yeah," added Andy. "Kev's Dad has said we can use his barbecue. If we leave it down to Kev then we're all going to end up in A and E with food poisoning."

I laughed. "Surely his cooking isn't that bad?"

"You're kidding me." Andy laughed as he spoke. "Last time he cooked sausages they were grim. It was like biting through coal."

I pulled my face. "Doesn't sound the best."

"It wasn't," Claire butted in. "I could have used them as a new medium for my art project." I laughed again. Surprised that I found her genuinely funny. I was starting to relax. As soon as Claire showed some interest in inviting me Amy changed her attitude.

"Yeah, Hope," Amy spoke in a sickly-sweet voice. "Why don't you come? There are loads of people from our year going, kind of a reunion. Dad is always talking about how hard you work. You deserve to have a little fun."

'But Helen.' My mind screamed at me. 'You can't leave Helen.'

"It's a nice offer," I replied. Pleased that they had asked me. "But I have to go back home."

Mike appeared behind me. He had a bottle of wine in his hand.

"Go with them." Mike coaxed. "Your Mum won't miss you for one night." He handed me a bottle of wine. "This is a little something from me." He told me. "To say thank you for being my best worker and to say congratulations for getting such amazing results."

Tears filled the corners of my eyes. "Oh, Mike!" I exclaimed. "Thank you."

"Don't get too carried away." He laughed. "It's just a bottle of wine." But I knew he understood. He was one of the very few people who had any idea about my home life. "Nip home and change then you can meet them all down at the beach. It's only about fifty yards from your house anyway."

I nodded. "Thank you." I looked around at the tables. "Well if you don't mind, once we're all cleared up?"

"Go now," Mike told me. "Emma will help me clear up."

The house was empty when I arrived back home. An empty vodka bottle stood on the kitchen worktop. It appeared that Helen had run out for supplies. Quickly I washed and changed into my faded blue shorts and a long white shirt. I untied my hair and tousled it. I applied a little lipstick and mascara. It felt good to be going somewhere for once. I was about to lock the front door behind me when a thought occurred to me. I slipped back into the lounge, found a sheet of paper and a pen and wrote a quick note. I folded the paper and wrote 'Mum' on the front before propping it against the clock on the mantelpiece. It felt strange to be addressing her as Mum. I almost went back to write Helen instead but decided to leave it as it was.

Gleefully I ran down the steps to the beach. The sun was just starting to kiss the sea.

The glow of the camp-fire drew me like a beacon. I was impressed by the effort that the gang had gone to. As well as the camp-fire there was an old beaten kettle barbecue. A few people had brought camp chairs. There were iceboxes full of beer sat in the sand at various points. A ghetto blaster took pride of place on a group of rocks overlooking the party. There must have been eighty people there. Many were sat on makeshift seating, from rocks to barrels to washed up driftwood. A group of ten or so lads were playing football. What they lacked in skill they more than made up for in enthusiasm. I approached the group a little nervously. Kevin appeared like the conductor of a band as he stood in front of the barbecue overlooking the scene. As he spotted me his face broke into a broad smile.

"Hope!" he exclaimed. "I was beginning to think you had got lost." I shook my head.

"I had to feed the cat." I lied. I didn't want to admit to being as nervous as I was about coming to the party.

"Grab a beer." He told me.

"Thanks." I walked over to the nearest icebox and pulled out a cold beer. I found a bottle opener on a small table next to the box and used it to free the lid from the bottle. I tasted the cold liquid. The bubbles danced excitedly on my tongue.

"Hope!" Amy shouted and waved. I looked over to her spot near the fire. She and Emma were sat together on a driftwood seat. Several empty bottles sat next to them on the sand. With concern, I wondered how many of them the girls had drunk. "Come and sit over here." Amy beckoned me manically.

Filled with uncertainty I walked around to their spot by the fire.

"Hi." I quietly greeted them as I sat down. "Cool party," I told them. That comment was a complete understatement. The party was so much

more than a cool party for me. This was acceptance after years of feeling like an outsider.

I sat down in front of the fire. The heat was stinging my bare legs, but I didn't want to move them. My fingers slipped into the warm sand. I closed my eyes as music from the blaster washed over me. My head was spinning slightly, the beer I had drunk had numbed my senses slightly, but I felt happy. I was overcome with the feeling that this was what life was for. It wasn't for studying, or for working hard, or for clearing up after your mother. Life was for sitting on the beach sipping beer and listening to crap pop songs. It was for feeling pretty and funny and all of the other things that people desired. I could hear Amy and Emma laughing and chatting and giggling. I had a sneaky feeling that they may have been laughing at me, but I wasn't sure and for the first time I didn't care. Kevin and Claire had been kind to me. Whatever Kevin or Claire did others would soon follow.

"We're going to go skinny dipping" Amy giggled, almost falling into the fire.

"Nooooo." I shook my head in disagreement and wagged my finger in a far too exaggerated fashion. "I think you might be a bit too drunk" I slurred.

"No such thing." She declared whilst lifting an already empty bottle to her lips.

I shook my head again. "You could fall over and drown."

"Then you'll have to come to save me."

"No chance! I'll fall over and drown."

"Kevin," She purred in her sexiest voice, "tell Hope she has to skinny dip with us."

His eyebrows raised and a playful smile tugged at the corners of his mouth.

"Skinny dipping?" He laughed, "Without me?" he winked in my direction. His face looked more handsome than ever in the glow of the warm fire, or perhaps that was the effect of the beer.

I could feel my cheeks redden and hoped that the glow from the fire would hide my embarrassment.

"No skinning dipping!" I raised my hand to signal no. "And that's final."

"Ok," Kevin nodded in agreement, "no skinny dipping." He stretched and started to stand up, I realised his intentions a second too late as he scooped my tiny body into his strong arms. He lifted me off the ground in one swift movement, "but you didn't say no to fully clothed dipping!" he laughed as he started to saunter towards the sea. I squirmed in his arms, but he only held me closer, his muscular body felt firm and strong against mine.

I could smell aftershave mingled with the scent of him, I felt a tingle of desire. The sound of music started to drift into the distance and I could hear soft waves lapping onto the shore. The salt of the sea mingled with the scent of Kevin. He was chuckling to himself as we got closer to the sea, by now the suns descent was almost complete. The sea and the horizon glowed orange as the sun burnt its way out of the sky. He inhaled as his feet splashed through the cold water, wading in until I could feel the cold liquid splashing against my spine. I squealed with nervous anticipation of what was to come.

"Are you ready?" He lifted me higher ready to throw me into the icy water.

"No!" I squealed, giggling nervously.

I expected to be enveloped, I expected him to plunge me in, regardless of my protests. Instead, he turned around on the spot and started to wade back to the shore.

"Come here then," his voice was almost a whisper as he gently lowered me to the ground, feet first. He pulled me close to him, his arms around my waist. The water was lapping at my ankles, the sand soft and wet between my toes. I closed my eyes in anticipation of his kiss. I could feel the sparks of passion before our lips even met. His lips were soft and warm against mine. His body firm in complete contrast. Nervously I raised my hand to touch his chest, shivers were sent through my spine as our bodies pressed closer, his tongue tasting my lips, hands caressing my body. I didn't want the kiss to end. It felt perfect. A first kiss by the sea as the sunset. Shakespeare sister drifting through the air "Stay with me..." the lyrics played through my mind as I returned his kiss. I could have stayed there all night. I could have kissed him forever. Yet a nagging thought came into my mind. The thought that was never too far away. I pulled away gently, my eyes fluttered open and I glanced up to meet his gaze. I smiled.

"I have wanted to do that for so long." He pushed a strand of hair behind my ear as he spoke.

"Throw me in the water?" I teased.

"Kiss you." His lips met mine again. I relished the kiss for a second or two before I slowly pulled away. I smiled to show he had done nothing wrong.

"You didn't know I existed." I laughed.

"Oh, I did." His voice was deep and full of sincerity. "I've always wanted to do that, ever since primary school."

I was amazed, I didn't think Kevin remembered me from our tiny primary school.

"When Miss Walker would always send you outside for pratting around?" I laughed as I remembered his love/ hate relationship with our third-year junior teacher. He could charm himself out of trouble in no time.

"You're not like other girls," Kevin spoke softly.

"That's always been my problem," I told him, pretending to joke. We both knew it was no joke.

"You never just follow the crowd for the sake of it. You're different. I like that."

"That doesn't help when I'm home alone every night," I told him.

"Your time will come." He touched my cheek as he spoke. "When all of the clones are married with a couple of kids and twice the size they are now, they'll realise that being different is a good thing."

"I want those things too," I replied. "Maybe not being twice the size, but I want to get married, have kids." I looked down at the water still washing around my feet. "I've never been part of a family, not a real one. For me having a family who loves you is immeasurable."

"Well, we only just kissed for the first time," Kevin winked at me, "but maybe in time."

I giggled with embarrassment, cringing inwardly.

His hand reached for my chin. He cupped my face and coaxed my lips towards his. As our lips softly brushed against one another I closed my eyes. The softness of his lips pushing against mine felt delicious. His hand gently held my head. Our bodies pressed against each other as we kissed, barely aware of the waves lapping at our legs.

When we parted I sighed and rested my head against his chest. I was breathing heavily. Dizzy with the feelings that his kiss had aroused. I looked back towards the shore in a cloud of happiness. The campfire was starting to fade. Silhouetted figures danced in the sand. My line of sight followed the steps back up to the clifftop. I looked towards my little house, the porch light calling me home. I felt a pang of guilt when I thought of Helen all alone. I wondered if she had found my note.

"I have to go," I told Kevin with a sudden urgency. He followed my gaze towards the house.

"You know you're the kid, right?" he tried to laugh at his own joke, but we both knew it wasn't funny.

"I'll walk you home"

I nodded. "I'd like that."

We sauntered home hand in hand. I felt as though I was bouncing on a cushion of air, like the boy from the film the snowman I was walking through the air. Kevin was my guide.

As we neared the house I started to dawdle, rooting through the pockets of my cut off jeans for my keys. I wanted Kevin to kiss me again. I was anticipating the taste of his lips, my spine-tingling. I couldn't shake the feeling that there was something amiss as I neared the cottage. The porch light was on. The door was slightly ajar. I felt my legs go weak. Cat paw prints glistened in the light of the porch. I stopped dead in my tracks, clasping Kevin's hand tightly. Maisy the cat sat at the front door licking her paws, her mouth stained red.

"I'm coming in with you." Kevin dragged me towards the house. I felt sick.

"Helen?" I shouted out, pushing open the door, but I knew there would be no reply. Bright red paw prints littered the hall. I walked to one side deliberately avoiding them, Kevin closely followed.

"Helen?" I shouted again, then with less certainty "Mum?" panic was taking over. I ran through the kitchen, ignoring the empty vodka bottles. I ran into the sunroom. Helen's favourite place to hang out. I saw the red pool before I saw her slumped on the sofa. Maisy's paw prints scattered through the pool. I had never seen so much blood.

"Call an ambulance," I screamed. I ran to my mother and threw my arms around her. I pressed against her wrists to stop any more blood escaping. Had it been possible I'd have scooped up the blood from the floor and poured it back into her. She felt cold and grey. Grasping her lifeless body in my arms, I buried my face into her hair.

"What have you done?" I yelled. "What have you done?" my whole body heaved as I sobbed for the mother who had never been a mother. "What have you done?"

I didn't hear the ambulance arrive. A pair of arms scooped me up and ushered me into the kitchen. I hardly knew where the blanket that I was wrapped in came from. I was dazed and confused, barely able to process the events of the evening. A hot drink was pressed into my hands and I sipped obediently at the hot, sweet tea. I could hear muffled voices, but nothing registered in my brain. I was aware that Kevin was in the kitchen and that another person kept coming and going. I didn't know what to think. How had this happened? How had I let this happen?

Eventually, it was just Kevin and me. He sat at the kitchen table, his eyes trying to meet my vacant stare.

"Hope." He spoke in a kind, soft voice. I could quite easily have fallen in love with him that night, maybe I did a little.

I looked up, instinctively brushing at my hair with my hand, feeling the now cold, gooey liquid that was covering me. I looked at my hand and saw the darkening blood. My mouth fell open in a fresh wave of shock.

"Hope." He spoke again, this time a little more firmly. I looked at him this time. My eyes met his, he looked away. Maybe the pain in my eyes was too much to bear, or maybe he felt ashamed that he had kissed a wretched creature such as me. "The ambulance crew want you to follow."

"Oh?"

"Yes." He spoke again. "You're in shock. They need to see you, but they said you could get cleaned up first."

"Oh." Was all I could manage. I started to stand but my legs almost gave way beneath my weight. Kevin jumped up to steady me.

"Come on, let's get you to the shower."

He walked with me through the hall and into the bathroom, careful to avoid the bloody prints that Maisy had left behind. He found a towel and laid it by the side of the bath. He turned on the shower, carefully checking that the water wasn't too hot or too cold. His hand brushed my cheek. "I'll be right outside. Call me if you need anything."

I stood and passively for what seemed like hours and allowed the water to wash over me. My head dizzy and fatigued. When the water started to run cold, I was shocked into some sort of consciousness. I wrapped myself in the towel and dried myself quickly. I became more aware of my surroundings. Of Kevin sat on the floor in the hallway, his back propped against the wall. I felt so much gratitude for the kindness he had shown me.

My bare feet slapped against the tiled floor of the bathroom as I walked towards the door.

"All done?" Asked Kevin as I stepped into the hall. I felt conscious of my naked body, thinly veiled by the towel.

"Yes, thank you." I smiled. "I'll be fine now thanks Kev."

"I'm coming with you to the hospital." He insisted. "Just go and throw on some jeans or something and we'll go. I've ordered a taxi. It should be here in about ten minutes."

I slipped on a pair of faded blue jeans and a jumper. As I stared at my reflection in the mirror I knew this would be the last time that I would see this room. I sighed as I pulled my suitcase and backpack from under my bed. They had been sat there for weeks. Packed and ready to go. I had just been waiting for my calling card. I think it had just arrived.

"I've called Jo-Jo," I told Kevin as I returned to the hall. A fleeting look of disappointment flashed across his face. "She's going to take me to the hospital, she's been like a mother to me over the years."

He nodded. I could see sympathy in his eyes. I didn't want sympathy. I wanted the passion I had felt only a few hours previously. I wanted to be free of this curse. Of the endless glances from neighbours. Of the murmurs of "poor thing" or "weirdo" as I walked past.

Everyone in the village knew what Helen was. So many people in the town viewed me with suspicious eyes, waiting for me to follow in my mother's faulted footsteps.

"Thank you," I spoke softly to Kevin. "Thank you for tonight." I imagined that he thought I was thanking him for helping with Mum, for waiting with me and for being so supportive. For all of those things, I was incredibly grateful. But I wanted to thank him for the party that he had invited me to. I wanted to thank him for the playfulness, the normality of the evening. The kisses we had shared. Those things were in some way better than support. I was used to people being supportive, Jo-Jo, Mike, teachers at school to a lesser extent. But I wasn't that used to being treated like a normal person. That felt good. I wanted to be treated like that all of the time and there was only one way to get there.

"You go now," I kissed Kevin on the cheek. I knew it would be the last time I would see him. "you have been the most wonderful support, I can't thank you enough, but I'm going to be fine now."

He protested, but I insisted. When the door closed behind him I felt such sadness. "As one door closes," I thought to myself.

23

The hotel room was eerily peaceful. I was lost in my thoughts following my encounters with Jon and Kevin.

I felt a pang of loneliness. Ben found his way into my thoughts. I missed him so much that I ached.

I picked up my phone. I had left it on charge in my room, deliberately avoiding the temptation to call Ben. I turned on the phone and looked at the screen. I had notifications for WhatsApp, Messenger and SMS. I sighed as I started with WhatsApp.

From Ben

3:32 am - Hope just come home. Whatever I've done I'm sorry.

Angrily I thought of him stood in bemusement surrounded by everyone he knew, wondering what on earth he had done to send his crazy wife off into a storm.

9:03 am - Call me

9:58 am - I'm worried about you. I've been worried about you since we lost the baby. You just don't seem to be able to function. It's as though a part of you died that day. A precious part. A part I can't manage without. I think you're punishing us for losing the baby, as though that's not punishment enough. I think you've forgotten why we're so great together.

I sat down on the soft bed with one huge sigh. I wanted to be angry with him. My anger was fuelling me, pushing me onwards. I had energy and drive for the first time in weeks, the one thing I didn't have was direction. I was lurching around looking for answers. In truth, I didn't know the question.

I laid the phone on the bedside table. I would look at the rest of the messages. I would respond. Right now, it was late. I was exhausted by my day. I laid my head on the soft pillow. Sleep took me in its arms and whispered dreams in my ear.

I sat on the tiled floor of the sunroom. My tiny legs were crossed as I reached for the colourful Lego blocks I needed to build my house. Besides me Faith sat, mirroring my position.

"My tower will be tallerer and betterer." I told her. She just smiled.

"I miss you," she whispered. The pain the words evoked shocked me.

"I miss you too," I replied. "I wish you were here with me."

"Don't trust the butterflies." Her blunt words filled me with foreboding.

"I don't like butterflies." I looked around as I whispered, checking that they weren't listening.

"They're enchanted." She told me.

My body lurched itself from sleep, arms and legs flailing as I fought to escape its clutches. My mouth cracked as I licked my dry lips. My throat was dry and scratchy. Terrified, I pulled the covers around me. I felt dizzy and confused.

"Go away," I shouted into the night, remembering what Helen had taught me to do when I had these dreams. "Go away, I'm too old for an imaginary friend." My face went numb, the blood drained away. A half-formed question took over my thoughts. Why had Helen taught me to push away the memory of my imaginary friend?

I wandered through town in a nostalgic haze. The sun was casting its hazy light through the streets giving them a picture-postcard feel. Walking through the town felt like a dream. I popped into a few shops to view their local souvenirs, all made in China. I followed the path down to the harbour and sat on the peer. Dreamily watching fishing boats departing. A family of seals were swimming around some of the boats, waiting eagerly for discarded offerings.

Eventually, I plucked up the courage to head for The Catchers Keep. I smiled as I saw the old chesterfield armchair by the door. The armchair was older than me. The blue leather had cracked and faded over time. As I sat down the seat did little to support me. By rights, this should have been the most uncomfortable seat in the place, but for me, it was choc chip ice-cream and a warm embrace wrapped into one. I could picture Jo-Jo sat across the table asking me about my day as we stopped off one the way home from school. When Jo-Jo took me for ice-cream it usually meant trouble. It usually meant that Helen had done something bad.

~

"How are you feeling?" The memory of Jo-Jo spoke in my mind.

An eight-year-old me tasted the sharp mint ice-cream, eyes wide. "He won't come back, will he?" I asked.

"He won't come back." She replied softly. "I promise."

I thought of the man who had been in the house the night before. Helen had brought him back from the pub. I should have been in bed, but I wasn't asleep and I heard Helen and Jo-Jo talking. I crept out into the hallway and wandered to the back of the house where I could hear voices. In the kitchen, Jo-Jo stood poised by the back door. Her face was stern. Helen was sat on the worktop. Next to her stood a man I had never seen before. I closed my eyes and made a wish that he would be nice to Helen. He was tall and broad with a short neck and a tight-fitting white T-shirt. His nose was crooked and his eyes were too close together. I didn't trust him. Just looking at him made me uneasy. Helen's arm was draped around his shoulders. Every time she spoke, she patted him casually with the other hand. Helen was being nice to Jo-Jo, she was always nice when she wanted something. She smiled a lot. I couldn't make out what they were saying. Helen said "Thank you." a couple of times. I heard "I'll be fine."

Jo-Jo said, "If you're sure." As she turned and closed the door behind her before heading to her own little cottage.

"Interfering busy body." The man with the crooked nose was loud. His voice was deep and gruff. Instantly I disliked him.

"She's just looking out for me." Helen took hold of his shoulders and turned him around. He put his hands on her hips as she bent forward to kiss him. I froze to the spot, too terrified to move yet repulsed by the sight of my mother kissing this strange man. As he lifted her shirt up over her head, I knew my being there wasn't right. As quietly as I could I turned around and tiptoed away. I was sure they would hear my heart pounding in my chest before they heard my toes stepping on the tiles. I felt my body being lifted from the ground in one swift movement.

"Nosey little freak." Disorientated the words confused me. Before I could fight or protest or begin to comprehend what was happening, I felt my body hitting the wall.

"Leave her." Helen ran to my defence. She stood protectively over me. "Go to your room and lock the door." The urgency in her voice frightened me. Shocked I was rooted to the spot. "Now!" She shouted as huge hands lifted her from the ground leaving me exposed.

"The village slut and her fucking freak kid." His voice bellowed angrily. I bolted. My feet slipping on the tiled floor as I scrambled down the hall. I saw the phone in the hall, I knew that Jo-Jo would help if I called her. I wanted to call her too, but he was so big and so angry and I was so afraid.

The banging and shouting went on for what seemed like an eternity. My mother's sobs and cries for help were pitiful. I tried desperately to open the window, to creep out to Jo-Jo, but it was stuck solid. My hands worked to free the frame to no avail. I was angry with myself for being weak. I was angry that I wasn't big enough or strong enough to fight back.

I sat against my bedroom door listening. Hot tears rolled down my face and dripped onto the wooden floorboards.

"I've heard all about that freak kid of yours." The man with the crooked nose bellowed. "Nosey little shit, always creeping around and watching, never saying Jack shit to anyone."

"She's a good kid." I was surprised to hear Helen defending me. "She was doing no harm, just heard us talking so came out to see what was going on."

"Came to see the show her slut mother was going to put on for her," he spat the words as though they were poison in his mouth, "I give it five years before she's more of a whore than you." I heard the cold thud of flesh hitting flesh. Helen suppressed a scream.

"Just go." Her voice filled with tears and pain.

"Fuck you, just go?" The anger in his voice was tenable. "I'm fucking getting what I came here for you fucking whore."

"No!" Helen's voice was tight and filled with pain.

I pushed my hands over my ears, desperate not to hear the sounds that were coming from the hall.

"Scratch me? You fucking whore!" Followed by a loud 'thwack'.

The sound of Helen's wails were heart-breaking. Eventually, the begging stopped. After that, there was just crying and animalistic grunts.

The sound of the front door slamming shut felt like freedom. Tentatively I opened my door and peered out into the hall. Helen lay with her head against the wall. Her legs were splayed apart, her skirt was pushed up leaving her exposed. Her nose was bleeding and her eye beginning to blacken. I grabbed the blanket from my bed. As I covered her exposed body she sobbed uncontrollably.

"Are you OK Mummy?" I asked naively.

"I'm so sorry." She told me.

"Please don't let any more men come here," I whispered as I cradled her like a baby.

She shook her head violently.

"I'm so sorry baby." She told me, looking into my eyes. "You deserve so much more than this. So much more than me."

~

"Hi." A perky voice broke me from my thoughts.

I looked up to see a pretty girl, maybe around sixteen. Her curly red hair was tied into pigtails. She wore cut off dungarees and a green T-shirt that didn't quite match. The apron around her waist and name tag told me that she worked here.

"Hi." I smiled, reaching for the menu with the other. "Could I just have a latte, to begin with, please?" I requested.

"No problem." Gillian jotted on her pad and then was gone. I smiled. She seemed a quirky little thing. I guessed that she was Mike's current project. He liked to take on someone who needed a job, a role model, maybe even a father. He would fulfil all three needs. That's how it was with me. He would give me fatherly advice. He would guide me. He would build me up, encourage me and tell me how amazing I could be. I loved Mike for that.

I was halfway through my latte when I spotted Mike. He had popped out of the kitchen to show Gillian how to change the till roll. He was calm and patient. Gillian was anxious and flustered. A round lady with a deep frown stood at the counter, adding to Gillian's nerves. Mike flashed the lady a broad grin as he handed her the change.

"Sorry, we kept you waiting." Her frown softened ever so slightly. "We all have to learn hey?" The round lady smiled in return then thanked him. She looked through her change before throwing a handful of coins into the tip jar.

"Have a lovely day." She spoke directly to Gillian.

"Thank you so much," Gillian responded happily. "You too!"

I was afraid that Mike would disappear again before I could speak to him, but he was waiting until the lady had left before returning to his little kitchen. He looked around the cafe, rather like the captain of a ship surveying the waves to establish if they were in for a bumpy ride. When his eyes fell onto my seat his expression changed. Surprise and happiness filled his face. As Mike made his way over to me, I studied his face. Mike had been around my age when I saw him last, but he had aged well.

His hair was peppered with white. His eyes cracked when he smiled, but he was trim and healthy and a handsome man.

"Hope!" He took my hand and lifted me from my seat, flinging his arms around me in a warm embrace. He held on for longer than I had expected. When we parted he looked disappointed.

"Hope." He repeated with sadness, as though he couldn't quite believe that I was here before him.

"Good to see you." I smiled, hoping to keep things casual.

"Kevin said he saw you, but I could barely believe it." Was that a tear in his eye? It must be the sun stinging his eyes.

"Yes, I saw Kev last night." I laughed a little. "He saved me from a lecherous loser. He was like a knight in shining armour." I laughed trying to brush off what had happened the night before.

I wanted to avoid the inevitable questions. The 'where have you been?' 'Why did you go?' 'Why didn't you tell anyone you were safe?'

The truth was that I didn't feel as though there was anyone left to tell. As much as I loved the place, Port Merdow was so lonely when you didn't quite fit.

"Kevin said you're an architect," Mike spoke with awe.

I nodded. "I think I have you to thank for that," I told him with a wry smile. "You encouraged me." I paused and thought of all the times I had sat in the café doing course work because I knew that I wouldn't be able to do it at home. The times that Mike had built me up and told me how brilliant I was, how brilliant I could be. "You did so much Mike."

"You didn't need much encouragement." His eye wrinkled as he smiled. "You just needed someone to tell you they believed in you."

I nodded and smiled. Quite unsure what to say next. I felt a little awkward. Over twenty years had passed. I had once loved this man like a father, but that was a lifetime ago. I had changed. I wasn't the same little girl I was back then. Although I was damaged and bruised, I wasn't his pet project.

"This place has stayed the same," I told him, looking around at the dated decor as I recognised my faux pas. "I always loved this place." I corrected myself.

"Jo-Jo used to bring me when I was little." Mike nodded. "Is she still about?" I asked cautiously. I needed to know, but I was afraid of the answer.

"She's in the care home over by West Point." A fleeting sadness filled his eyes. "She's still the same old Jocee, but she struggles on her feet and she had a couple of falls..." He trailed off. I was elated. Yes, it was sad that Jo-Jo was in a care home, but she was alive. If she had passed without me having the opportunity to see her again then that would have been such a regret for me.

"Have you seen her?" I asked, sipping absently at my latte.

"I call over once or twice per week, keep her up to date on the local gossip." A smile played at the corners of his mouth. He always teased his aunt about being an old gossip. "She's still the same, always taking care of everyone."

"I see you followed in her footsteps." I nodded towards Gillian as she struggled with plates and cups, her uncoordinated body struggling to balance the load. "You always liked to take care of those who needed it." I winked with a lop-sided smile. Referring to all of the times he would give me much needed help, advice and guidance.

"Gillian is a great girl." Immediately he jumped to her defence, I loved him so much for that.

"She seems fab." I smiled knowingly. "Very unique."

"Some of the girls in her school have been giving her a hard time." He told me sadly. "I saw them all in here one afternoon. Offered her a job there and then."

"So, when are you going to hang up your apron?" I asked.

He shook his head. "You know I love this place too much."

We sat in silence for what seemed like an eternity. I had so many questions buzzing around in my head yet I couldn't decide what to ask. I decided to stick to Jo-Jo for now.

"Do you have the details?" I asked, looking up from my hands that had been absently twirling a napkin. "For Jo-Jo. I'd like to go and see her. Do you think she would mind?"

"I think she would mind if you didn't go over." He darted up to grab an order book and pen. He jotted down the address and phone number on a sheet then ripped it off and passed it to me.

"Thank-You." I smiled again. My brows furrowed as I tried to find a way to ask my next question. The question that had often occurred to me. The question that I thought I knew the answer to.

"Mike," he looked up as I spoke his name, "why were you so kind to me?"

He looked shocked, maybe confused by the question. I wasn't sure if he understood the deeper question within my words.

"You're giving me far too much credit." He told me with a smile. "I just needed a dedicated worker, someone who would work hard." We both knew he had done more than that, but I accepted his reply. He paused, looking at me fondly. "It's good to see you all grown up and more amazing than you ever believed you could be. An architect, for that Eco firm."

I smiled as he spoke, slightly uneasy at hearing the praise.

"I looked it up online." I blushed as he told me. "You're not just an architect, you have done wonders for that firm. You took an architect's firm that just did a little bit of environmental stuff and you changed it completely. It was your drive that got them to start installing geothermal heating. Those passive houses that you designed are amazing."

I laughed with embarrassment. “You can tell my husband created the web site,” I said in an attempt to brush off his compliments.

“He’s a lucky man.” I felt a stab of guilt as I thought of Ben. I doubted he felt very lucky at the moment. I still hadn’t responded to his messages, he would be worried. I didn’t want to worry anyone, I just wanted some space. I needed to unwrap my emotions and to truly understand who I was.

“Not recently,” I confessed. “Things aren’t too great at the moment, I think I’m running away again.”

I didn’t tell Mike about the miscarriage, about the conflict it had caused between Ben and I. I didn’t talk about the party or my journey down to Port Merdow.

“Talk to him.” His voice was full of hopeful determination.

I shrugged.

“What do you have to lose Hope?” I wanted to protest. I wanted to list the risks involved in making that call, of laying it all on the line, but when I tried to put it all into words none of it made sense. Right now, I was alone. My marriage was in tatters. I hadn’t been into work for weeks. My life in Chester was falling apart. Instead of facing it head-on I had run away. I wasn’t the same damaged eighteen-year-old that I had been then.

“I’m afraid,” I said quietly, suppressed tears threatening to spill from my eyes.

“What are you afraid of?” His voice was gentle and tender and everything that I remembered. My eyes met his. I held his gaze for a moment.

I shrugged. My thought hanging unspoken in the air. ‘What if I’m just like her?’

24

Having said my goodbyes to Mike, I wandered down to the beach. I sat on the sand and allowed the tide to tickle my bare toes. The water was icy cold, but it reminded me I was alive. I sat quietly contemplating my conversation with Mike. He had such a calm and confident manner. I doubted he had ever been afraid in his life. I knew he was right. I knew I needed to speak to Ben, I just wasn't sure what I would say.

I frowned at my stubborn streak and tried to push it away. 'What good is there in pretending you don't need anyone?' The thought ran through my mind without an answer. I was reminded again of the row that Ben and I had in the lift.

~

After our row in the lift shortly after my thirtieth birthday a whole week had passed before I plucked up the courage to go and speak to Ben. I had decided that I would apologise for jumping to conclusions. I didn't know how I would go about it, but I wanted to tell him that I found it difficult to trust people, especially men. I wanted to tell him how much I loved him. How he was always in my thoughts. No matter what I did I would think 'I wonder what Ben would think of this.' I longed to share our beautiful connection.

I found Ben sat at his desk in the second-floor office, exactly where I expected to find him. His brow was furrowed, his face full of concentration. He looked so sexy.

"Hi," I spoke tentatively. Afraid of his reaction. He looked up from his screen briefly and gave a cold half-smile.

"Hello."

"Ben, I err." I tried to find the words to start the conversation but I couldn't find what I wanted to say. "I err," 'I miss you, I love you, I'm sorry' my mind shouted. "I have a problem with AutoCAD on my PC." I managed feebly.

"Oh?" His voice was cold, his face looked sad and disappointed. "You'll have to log it, Trev will come and take a look when he gets a moment." Ben never made me log anything, he always came to my rescue whenever I needed help. To add insult to injury he was going to send Clever Trevor!

"Log it?" I questioned.

"You know the procedure." He shrugged. "Besides, when I'm down in Birmingham you'll have to stick to Protocol, none of this queue-jumping business then."

"Birmingham?" I repeated in confusion.

"Yep."

"You're going to Birmingham?"

"See," he looked me straight in the eye, "I always said you were smart."

"How long for?" I wondered if he sensed the disappointment in my voice.

"It's difficult to tell" He was doing his best to appear unphased, but I suspected it was all an act. "Richard wants to streamline the business, he says that IT has grown too big. They're moving me over to the Birmingham office in order to find cost savings."

"You didn't mention it." I sounded like a child, but I didn't care.

"I wasn't going to go." He shrugged slightly. "But if I stay here then Trevor and I have to fight it out to see who can stay in a job."

"But there's no way Richard would choose Trevor over you!" I protested.

"Exactly." He replied. I furrowed my brow.

"Exactly what?"

"Trevor has a wife and kid to think about," he looked up as he spoke. "They have another on the way too. How can I put that poor bastard out of work?" I wanted to hug him there and then. I wanted to tell him that he was amazing, instead, I stood watching him with unspent tears in my eyes.

"What about us?" My voice cracked as I spoke.

"There is no us." He was blunt and cold. "You made that abundantly clear."

"I thought we were friends."

He sighed deeply, as though it was all just too much effort.

"Hope I have been your friend since the first day we met. I introduced you to my family, I invited you to come and meet my football mates. We go everywhere together and we do everything, well almost everything." He added bitterly. "We're a couple in every way but one, but you're the only one who can't see that." He picked up a job sheet from the printer. "You're so busy looking for reasons for people not to love you! You just can't see the reasons people do love you. Until you learn to love yourself then I think we just need a little distance"

The voice in my head was screaming. Telling me to tell him to stop. I wanted to tell him that I loved him, but the words were stuck in my throat. "I don't want to lose you." Was all I could manage. It seemed woefully inadequate, but it was all I had.

"Why?" His question was like a slap in the face. I stared at him, my mouth hung open but no words escaped. "Give me one reason to stay."

"Can we still be friends." I wanted to turn back the clock to how it had been, how we had been before the kiss. I wanted us to sit and eat pizza together discussing which superpower we would choose, what colour love was or what people called barn owls before there were barns.

Ben sighed again. "If all we can ever be is friends then I'll settle for that."

25

I sighed. For what seemed like the thousandth time I wondered how different things might have been if Ben had not moved away when he did. Would we have got together sooner? Would we have avoided the trouble we had and conceived our baby sooner? I had read so much about miscarriage in the past few weeks. Everything pointed to my age being the cause. The burden of this factor played on my mind. I knew that I wanted to have a baby, but I also knew that I didn't ever want to risk another miscarriage. It would feel so wrong to make another life and condemn it to die.

With tears in my eyes, I stood up, picked up my sandals and bag and started to wander along the beach towards the road. I felt wretched. Not for the first time, I had more questions than answers.

I walked back through the cobbled streets on my way back to the hotel. Memories of distant times played through my mind. Trips down the main street holding hands with Jo-Jo as we chatted about my day at school. Memories of the errands that Helen would ask me to run, calling at the bakery for hot Cornish pasties when she was too hungover to make lunch. It felt like a thousand years had passed since I had walked through these streets, another life. Yet at the same time, it felt like only yesterday. I felt like the same vulnerable girl I had been back then. People pointing and staring. Each with an opinion about my mother and I. Some would show a little kindness, but most would avoid me if they could.

I stopped outside an art shop. Gazing through the window at the various scenes from local artists. There was a pretty range of oil paintings that had been created by the same artist. I smiled fondly as I recognised the harbour. Several paintings had been created from slightly different angles in slightly different light. In one the sun was dreamily dipping into the sea, casting its orange light over the water. In others, children played merrily with buckets and spades. I smiled inwardly as I remembered my own adventures around the harbour and the beach. How Jo-Jo would take her book of sea creatures down on to the sand and the two of us would scour the rock pools to see what we could find. We would carefully place the creatures into buckets full of water then search Jo-Jo's book in the hope of identifying our finds. Afterwards, we would always take care to return the animals to their homes. Jo-Jo would be kind and patient. She would remind me to be gentle. I loved being around Jo-Jo so much. She made me feel safe. I didn't often feel that way.

Behind the oil paintings, there were some pretty watercolours by a different artist, I spotted a Kerry Darlington and smiled. I loved her work so much. I was about to walk away when another painting caught my eye. A soft watercolour, eerily familiar. I knew I had not seen this painting before, but I knew the work. Instinctively I knew from the shapes and the brush strokes, the way the colours blended. I had to have a closer look.

The bell rang as I opened the door. A young girl, probably about eighteen sat at the till texting. She looked up briefly and smiled as I entered the shop, then returned her attention to the phone in her hand.

I was drawn towards the painting that I had spotted through the window. A small watercolour, in a plain black frame, mounted on a white background. The painting was of a meadow, filled with wildflowers. In the centre of the image, a brightly coloured butterfly sat on a flower. Wings outstretched as though it was about to take flight. There were dozens of butterflies in the air, but none as magical looking as the one in the centre of the painting. I knew before I checked for the signature what it would say. H. Tegan, the N extended to form a swirl under her name. How? Perhaps she painted this before I was born? It looked different from the work I was familiar with. Simpler, less tortured. Maybe she had created this when she was happy before I came along and ruined her life?

"Excuse me?" I looked up and addressed the young lady behind the counter. She smiled.

"This painting?" I enquired. "Do you know anything about the artist?"

She sighed slightly as she placed her phone down and walked over. "We've had that one in a while I think." She pointed to the signature. "Helen Tegan." She told me. "A local I think, we've had her work before."

I felt numb. "Where did you get this?"

"I don't know." Replied the girl shrugging. "I just work here."

"Is there anyone who could tell me?" I asked.

"Henry would know," she offered, "but he's away at the moment."

"Away?" I repeated.

"Yeah, gone visiting family."

"Can you call him?" I asked, my voice starting to sound desperate.

The girl eyed me suspiciously. "Do you want the painting?" she asked, "It's only fifty pounds."

"I just need to know about the artist." My voice was starting to crack.

"I don't know, I only know she's local." She shrugged again. "Henry will be back next week, you can ask him then."

Exasperated I agreed to buy the painting and then call back the following week to talk to Henry. I was confused. Who had sold my mother's painting?

I returned to the hotel in a daze. I sat the painting on the dressing table and gazed at it. I gazed at the butterflies. Ben would be amazed if he knew I had bought a painting of a meadow full of butterflies. I was desperately frightened of them, I had been for as long as I could remember. Ben used to tease me about my fear until I told him the story of the store cupboard. It was incredibly rare for me to reveal anything of my past so this disclosure was even more important.

~

I was in the second year at junior school. Amy was in my class, but we barely spoke. I knew that Jo-Jo was related to her, but wasn't sure how. Amy would talk to me when nobody else was around, but in front of the other girls, she was vicious. She and the other girls would taunt me, they used to laugh when they made me cry. I stopped crying by the time I got to the junior school. Instead, I started to lash out.

It all started one lunchtime in late April. The sun was bright in the sky. Flowers had started to bloom. There was an air of excitement as the children were allowed out on the grass. We were told that we could go on the parts that had been cut, we could run around and play, sit and make daisy chains, but we were not to go into the wild meadow area. We had a new headteacher who was keen on the environment and part of the school fields had been planted with wildflower seeds. The grass was long and lush and made a great hiding place. I crept off alone and lay back amongst the tall grass. I looked up at the sky, watching a plane drifting across the sky leaving a fluffy vapour trail behind it. I wondered how it would feel to be lifted away, transported from the world I knew. How it would feel to leave this all behind. I thought of leaving Jo-Jo and that made me feel sad.

"You're not allowed over here!" The sound of Amy's voice jolted me from my thoughts. I looked up and saw Amy and Emma stood looking at me.

"Go away." I was disappointed by the unimaginative reply, but it would have to do.

"I'm going to tell Mr Rigby off you." She announced.

"You're going to do what?" I asked, then reminded myself that now was probably not the time to pick her up on her language skills.

"I'm going to tell him that you're spoiling his meadow." She sounded self-assured. I shot her a sideward glance.

"I'm just lay here minding my own business Amy," I protested, "just leave me alone for once in your fucking life."

"Oh my God!" Amy exclaimed in shock. "You swore."

"Amy please just leave me be," I asked again. "I'm not asking to hang out with you. I'm not trying to be part of anything, I know when I'm not wanted." I sat up and met her gaze, "Just let me live my life in peace."

"You're going to get done." She turned and started to march off towards the teacher in the middle of the yard.

I jumped up and lurched after her, grabbing for her arm. I held her tightly in my grip and pulled her closer to me. "Don't you dare," I spoke menacingly in her ear.

"Get off me." She squealed.

"It's about fucking time you learned to just leave me alone." I dragged her back and pushed her to the ground. I spotted the bright blue wings in my peripheral vision. I was filled with horror, my eyes grew wide. I staggered backwards brushing at the butterfly that had landed on my chest, blind panic had taken over me. As I fell to the ground I could see a sea of faces surrounding me laughing.

"Oh my god!" I heard one voice calling out. "It's only a butterfly" A chorus of laughter followed.

"She's frightened of butterflies." Again laughter. I scrambled to my feet and ran towards the school.

For weeks there was an air of tension around school. I did what I could to avoid Amy. Every now and then I would catch her pointing and giggling with her friends. I tried to hold my head high and walk away.

It was a Friday afternoon when it happened. We always had video time on Friday afternoons. Miss Begley would roll in a huge TV and video recorder from the store cupboard and would play a video. As we sat in anticipation, I hoped it would be "The Boy from Outer Space." I loved that program. I noticed that Amy and her friends were giggling and digging each other knowingly as the video started.

Miss Begley started the video and went out into the corridor to mark our books while we watched the show. Amy went out into the corridor. I could see her chatting to Miss Begley for a moment or two, then she returned to the classroom.

"Miss Begley wants you to give the exercise books out so we can make notes," Amy informed me. I was book monitor. I was proud when Miss Begley had asked me to be monitor. I always took my job seriously.

I went into the storeroom, leaving the door ajar to let in enough light to allow me to find the books.

The English exercise books were red and normally sat on the shelf on the right-hand side. Today the books weren't there. I turned to leave the store cupboard when a box was thrown to the ground. As the door slammed shut the last few rays of light shone on the box as a flurry of wings exploded from the box. I held in a scream. I screwed my eyes tight. In a panic I backed myself towards the door, pushing back against the pressure of dozens of tiny hands.

I turned around and pushed with my full weight. Forcefully trying to escape my prison. I slammed my fists against the door, each thud was more painful than the previous, the skin on my fists beginning to tear. I scratched and clawed like a wild animal, desperate to be free. I could feel the wings brushing against my face. Wildly I swiped at their tiny forms. Finally, I gave in. I curled in a ball on the floor. My arms covering my face. My whole body heaved with the sobs that engulfed me.

When Miss Begley found me, I was covered in blood and tears. My nails had broken from scratching the door. My fists and my fingers bled. I sobbed for hours, even once I was safe in Mr Rigby's office and waiting for Helen to collect me. I sat in the plastic seat, my knees pulled up to my chest. I sobbed. I couldn't help it.

I heard hushed voices in the corridor outside the office. I heard the word "strange" uttered a few times and "doesn't fit in" I think it was Miss Begley who said, "The mother is a right one." Once more I wished for the plane to carry me away. Anywhere had to be better than this.

26

I put the postcode for the address that Mike had given me into my Sat Nav. The arrival time would be ten thirty, give or take. I was excited to see Jo-Jo, but nervous at the same time.

As soon as I walked through the door of the lounge the smell of lavender hit me. The room was lined with pink PVC covered high backed chairs. A TV mounted on the wall was playing an antique show, but none of the residents seemed to be watching. Silence hung in the room like a nagging guilt. I searched the vacant faces for the woman who practically raised me. A woman I had not seen for over twenty years. I was about to turn and leave when I heard a soft chuckle. A smile touched my lips as I glanced toward the familiar sound. Our eyes met, the initial puzzlement in her expressive brown eyes soon turned to recognition. Her face became ashen. She was shocked to see my face, especially considering how I had left the town. I choked on the lump forming in my throat as I was suddenly confronted with the realisation of the pain I had caused. My eyes stung as tears began to gather. I clenched my jaw to stop them from building any further as I walked, almost ran towards Jo-Jo. She stood up just as I reached her and as I embraced her soft, cuddly frame the tears started to flow. I buried my face into her shoulder and sobbed as I held the kindest woman I have ever known. Emotions filled me up and pulled me in every direction. Regret, guilt, fear, happiness, a huge sadness. I was in turmoil, my heart bursting with love for this woman, yet the memories she evoked were almost too painful to stand.

I held her for only a minute or two, but time seemed to stand still as we embraced. When I let go we both slumped in the nearest chairs, staring at each other with disbelief. Both of us wiping away tears.

"Hope." Eventually, Jo-Jo spoke my name. The word was almost a whisper, almost a question, an exclamation of all of the lost time when I had been away, but such warmth was in her voice. "Hope." She spoke again, this time a little louder, a little clearer. A warm smile touching her eyes as she stared at me.

"Jo-Jo." My eyes met hers, tears brimming yet again. "Jo-Jo I'm so sorry…." As I started to speak, she gently raised her finger to her lips to gesture shhh.

"You're here." She cupped my hand in her soft warm clasp. "You're safe. That's all that matters."

I hadn't given much thought to those I had left behind when I left the town. I had simply needed to get away. To escape. Faced now with the turmoil I had left behind I realised how selfish I had been.

"Mike told me you were here. I wish I had come sooner." I said.

"The house was getting a bit much." This seemed to be her time to apologise. "I had a fall and did myself a bit of mischief," she chuckled half embarrassed. "I never planned to get so old." She winked.

"You're not old Jo-Jo, you're just about hitting your prime."

She chuckled again. The sound of her voice evoked warm memories of days at the beach and walks in the park. "Tell me about you! I want to know everything there is to know."

"I just don't know where to begin." That was the truth. I had so much to process, so many thoughts, so much pain. I knew I was running away from my present, but I knew I was also facing the past. I didn't know which would be more painful.

Jo-Jo was kind, as always. She listened as I told her about Ben. About the baby, about the miscarriage and the hurt that it caused, the way I had been angry towards Ben for not sharing my grief, how he seemed dismissive like it had been nothing. We both cried and we both laughed. We hugged some more. I made promises to visit again and I hoped I would. Jo-Jo was an amazing woman. She always made me want to be the very best version of me I could be. Even when I was messed up and in pain, I wanted to be better for her, because she deserved to be with the best version of everyone.

"I always wanted children of my own," Jo-Jo spoke softly at first, almost as though she was thinking out loud. "Steve and I tried, for years. I became pregnant at twenty-eight, I lost her at twenty-four weeks." A tear slipped down her cheek as she spoke, her eyes fixed on a vase of flowers on the windowsill as she spoke. "she was so tiny, her skin was almost red. Steve said she looked like a monster, he didn't want to touch or hold her, but to me she was beautiful. She was perfect in every way, she just wasn't strong enough for this world."

"Jo-Jo I'm so sorry." I gushed "I had no idea."

"If I could go back and change things so I had never been pregnant, never felt her moving inside me, responding to my touch, then I wouldn't. I wouldn't spare myself the pain for the love I felt for her. The purest love of all is the love that a mother has for her child."

"Not always." I frowned.

"Don't be so harsh towards Helen." Her eyes spoke of a truth hidden in plain sight. "Your mother loves you more than you will ever know."

"I can't." I shook my head. "Not today." I knew that was why I had come here. I knew I needed to face those demons. But I didn't feel strong enough.

"Where are you staying," Jo-Jo asked.

"Over at The Meadows." Jo-Jo wrinkled her nose with distaste. "I have a key for your Mum's house. Mike goes over there now and then to do odd jobs and make sure it's not falling apart."

"Really?" I asked in astonishment. "But surely it should have been sold?"

Jo-Jo looked puzzled. "Oh no." She protested. "That's not a decision any of us can make."

"So it just sits empty?" I was puzzled.

"Well, like I said, Mike keeps an eye on things." She looked as though she had more to say, more to add. We both felt the elephant in the room in equal measure. The way I had left had been wrong. I should have done it properly. I should have said my goodbyes.

The knowledge that I had not attended my own mother's funeral had been with me all this time. I thought of the last time I had been at the house. The image of Helen lay on the floor in a pool of her own blood flitted through my mind. I shook my head in alarm.

"I'm not sure if I could," I told her. "Not after what happened there."

"Take the key anyway." She delved into the handbag sat beside her chair. She looked at me with her warm eyes. "It's what your Mum would want." She uttered.

"Thank you, Jo-Jo." I stood up and hugged her.

"Did she have a name?" I asked as I turned to leave.

"My baby?" Jo-Jo asked. I nodded. "She was called Ellen."

"She had the best mum in the world," I told her.

27

I hadn't intended to call at Treth Chy on my way back to the hotel, at least that was what I told myself. A deep yearning in my heart was calling me there. As my car crunched over the gravelled driveway to my childhood home I was ready to turn and leave. I was overtaken by a cocktail of emotions. The house looked almost exactly as I remembered. The woodwork was worn and peeling in places and the lawn was overgrown. Weeds were peeping through the gravel. The old swing chair on the veranda sat empty, the seat faded. Stepping out of the car was like stepping into a dream of the distant past. Tears started to sting at my eyes, I felt a familiar choking in my throat. Should I turn and leave? The question turned into a thought, the thought was about to turn into an action when I caught a glimpse of the sea. The sight of that blue expanse mesmerised me. A cool breeze whispered over the clifftop.

The sight before me was beautiful. The sun was just taking its last breath of the evening before it sank beneath the deep blue waves. The horizon was illuminated by an array of red and orange light. Long dune grass on the clifftop was scattered with pretty wildflowers in yellows, blues and pinks. The grasshoppers had just started their evening romance calls. The sound filled the air. The scent of the salty sea mingled with the flowers. The sight, the sounds, the scent all chillingly familiar sent shivers through my body. I hugged my tiny body, trying to convince myself that it was just the cold. I slumped on the grass and closed my eyes. Panic started to rise within me as the thought of a thousand butterflies flitting about filled my mind.

Broken images from my childhood whispered in and out of my thoughts. I could picture the cliff top in mid-summer.

~

The sun was shining. The air was scented with sunscreen and ice cream. The sounds of children's voices were carried on the wind as they played on the beach far below. Flowers littered the cliff top. Hundreds of pretty butterflies danced from one bloom to another collecting nectar. To the three-year-old me the butterflies were bewitching fairies. Their pretty faces beaming as they danced around. I wanted to touch one, to hold it in my hand, to make a wish. The fairies spoke to me. They danced enchantingly through the air, enticing me to play. I reached for one, my legs carrying me a little faster, moving a little further away from my mummy. I knew she was behind me but the fairies wanted to play. I started to run, darting from one to another, hands stretched out. I reached for the pretty creatures, desperate to hold one in my hand. I almost caught one then giggled as it flitted away. "Stop". I heard my mother's voice floating through the wind. I could hear her feet thumping against the ground as she ran to catch up with me. I wanted the fairies. I wanted to be part of their world of magic and fun and freedom. I giggled as I flitted left as my mother grew closer. I liked this game. I saw the most beautiful blue creature perched on a yellow flower. Its wings were outstretched in a graceful pose, its long legs reminded me of the ballerinas I had seen on the television. Slowly I approached the magical being with a feeling of the awe and amazement. I reached out with my stubby arm, expecting the creature to flit away as the others had. The butterfly sat still on the bloom, waiting for me to play with it. I grabbed the butterfly with both hands, cupping it gently. Clasping the creature I proudly turned to find Helen. I wanted to share my find. A blood-curdling sound filled the air. I didn't recognise the scream that filled the air as my mother's voice. It chilled me to the bone. Terror overtook my body. I felt sick as tears sprang into my eyes. Every muscle in my body contracted. I became lost in the terror of that scream. The sound filled the air for an unthinkable time. I stood frozen to the spot, tears rolling down my chubby face. I searched the landscape for my mother. Pure terror lit up my heart when I saw her stood on the cliff edge. If she took another step, another inch, she would be gone, she would hit the rocks below and she would be killed. I knew because she had warned me so many times. She had told me how dangerous the cliffs were and how I shouldn't go near the edge. She had made it so clear, yet there she was. Stood on the clifftop screaming. I started to sob uncontrollably. "Mummy" I shouted, but she didn't seem to hear my voice. "Mummy come back" I shouted again. "It's dangerous Mummy, you could fall on the rock." Still, the screams filled the air. I sat down, feeling alone and afraid. Then I remembered. I opened up my hands and saw the butterfly squashed against my palm. New feelings of guilt and remorse filled me. For me now all magic was lost.

~

I opened my eyes, chilled by the uprising of my quashed memories. My fear of butterflies was starting to make sense. They reminded me of that day. They reminded me of my mother's breakdown.

I stood up, shivering in the sea breeze. I glanced towards the house. It was barely illuminated as the sun played its closing song for the night. I was disappointed when I found myself sat back in my car. I tried to tell myself I didn't want to disturb the neighbours. I made a thousand excuses in my mind about why I shouldn't go back into the house. I decided instead to treat myself to an evening meal out. I was growing tired of the limited hotcl menu.

28

I was met with raised eyebrows when I arrived at Mario's alone. The waiter sat me in the corner out of sight. I nibbled breadsticks while I waited for my order to be taken. I had spent ten minutes perusing the menu before choosing what I always had, fillet steak. I considered ordering the calamari as a starter but thought that might be overdoing it a little.

The restaurant was dimly lit and filled with couples. Swing music played gently in the background. I watched a young couple nearby as they stared into each other's eyes, sipping white wine and each laughing a little too enthusiastically at the others jokes. The smell of Italian food reminded me of Ben. I thought about the leaving do that Becky from finance had arranged before Ben moved to Birmingham. I got the feeling that she was interested in Ben, maybe that was just the green-eyed monster.

~

It was Derek who persuaded me to go along to Ben's leaving party. I arrived late at the restaurant having spent hours getting ready. I was determined to look my best.

The restaurant was smart and vibrant. It was dimly lit and smelled of tomatoes and oregano. As I waited to be seated, I drank in the atmosphere. The centre of the room was taken up by a dance floor. In the middle of the dance floor, a gleaming white grand piano stood on a tiny round stage. The singer sat at the piano had a look of Sinatra, but his voice wasn't as strong. I spotted the Eco Build group at the far end of the restaurant. From what I could tell most of the office had come out. Ben sat at the centre of the long table, his blonde mane shining like a halo in the candlelight. Oddly it looked like the De Vinci painting. I felt a pang of sadness. The waiter showed me to the table. I felt a little too tall stood next to him, it must have been the heels. The only seat left was at the far end of the table. I smiled as I sat down facing Trevor, trying to hide my disappointment.

Throughout the meal, Trevor talked about his motorbiking hobby. About his wife and her insistence that he should become vegetarian and how he still ate meat when she wasn't there and how tonight he was going to have a bloody big steak. I nodded and smiled in all the right places, but I longed to be at home, curled up with Maisy and a good book.

As the meal came to an end a few of the women wandered over to the dance floor, seemingly hoping to attract the attention of the Sinatra impersonator. I didn't notice Ben until his hand was on my shoulder. I did all that I could to keep the tears from my eyes. Warmth spread through me. I wanted to just sit here like this forever.

"Would you like to dance?" He whispered in my ear. I took his hand with a smile, desperate to hide the turmoil that was going on inside me.

Sinatra was singing Mack the Knife. I tried desperately to keep the rhythm but still felt foolish and uneasy. When the tempo changed Ben took hold of my hand and pulled me close to him. I smiled as I recognised 'Something Stupid' and wondered if it had been Ben's request.

I breathed in Ben's aftershave as he held me close. My spine tingled with anticipation. Just being close to him set my soul on fire. He sang in my ear, his voice out of key but beautiful to me.

"Ben I'm sorry." The words I had wanted to say for weeks erupted from my soul. "It's so hard for me to explain, there is so much I..." I paused, a little lost for words. "There's so much that has happened in my life." I managed. "I struggle to trust people." There, it was out. I hadn't given him the gory details, but I had told him it wasn't him.

"I know." He whispered quietly in my ear, his lips brushing my cheek as he spoke. "I know you struggle to trust people." I looked down to avoid

his gaze. "I wish I could help, I wish you could see yourself the way I see you." My eyes brimmed with tears.

"I don't want to lose you, Ben, you mean too much to me."

"I don't want to lose you either." His voice was kind and gentle.

"Can we be friends?"

"Best friends." He told me.

I rested my head against his chest and we swayed gently to the music.

~

I took my phone out of my handbag and unlocked the screen. I opened WhatsApp and clicked on Ben's name. My screen told me that Ben had been last on line five minutes earlier.

There were four unread messages.

Ben: I want you to know that no matter what, no matter how bad you think things are, we can fix this. Just come home.

07:30

Ben: Remember US. Remember why we love US

07:45

The next message was a photograph of Ben and I together. His hand was extended, holding the phone.

I smiled as I remembered our trip to Barcelona. We had sat drinking beer in a tiny bar, away from the crowded La Ramblas. Ben had held up his phone for a selfie, we both smiled fondly into the camera. The look on my face in that photograph was pure love and joy.

Ben: Remember lazy afternoons soaking in the bath.

Remember paddling in the sea at Blackpool.

Remember everything that is good about US.

07:58

I fought to keep the tears from my eyes. I wanted to fix things. I really did. Suddenly I wasn't hungry. The waiter still hadn't taken my order so I stood up, made my excuses and left. I guessed it looked like I had been stood up. Maybe twenty years ago this would have worried me, but today I had more on my mind.

29

Back at the hotel, I lay in bed. I felt more alone than ever. I closed my eyes. I pictured Ben. I imagined the way it felt when he touched me. I imagined his lips touching mine. I remembered fondly the first time we spent the night together.

Ben was still working in the Birmingham office, although we were in touch the distance had come between us. We had promised to remain friends, but it wasn't the same.

~

It was a Friday night. I got home from the office late. My apartment was in darkness when I arrived home. Immediately I felt that there was something wrong. The apartment was too quiet. Normally Maisy would greet me at the door, wrapping her tail around my legs as she brushed herself against me, almost tripping me up. Tonight she didn't greet me.

I searched the apartment calling her name. In a blind panic, I ran from room to room. I was reminded of the night of the party on the beach, returning home to find Helen.

I finally found Maisy in the bottom of my wardrobe. She looked like she was sleeping. I knew that if I reached out to touch her that her body would be stiff and cold. Silent tears rolled down my face. I felt helpless, afraid to move her, but afraid to leave her there. I paced up and down trying to decide what to do. I found a shoebox and decided to place her inside, but I just couldn't bring myself to put my hands around her lifeless body.

I dialled Ben's number without thinking. When he answered the call I cried.

"Ben, can you help me?" I croaked the words into the phone.

"Hope?" He asked tentatively.

"It's Maisy." I sobbed.

"The cat?" He asked.

"Yes." My voice was subdued.

"Do you need me there?" He asked without hesitation.

"Would you mind?" I started to feel guilty for asking.

"I don't mind." He replied. "Will you be ok until I get there?"

I glanced towards the bedroom and thought of poor Maisy curled up in the bottom of my wardrobe.

"I'll be fine," I said, although I wasn't sure how true that was.

While I waited for him to arrive I soaked myself in the bath. The warm water washing over me and helping to relieve the tension in my body. I blow-dried my long hair and applied a little makeup before putting on a pair of jeans and a jumper.

The doorbell rang a little before ten. When I opened the door to Ben I wrapped my arms around him and buried my head into his shoulder. He hugged me back and rocked me like a baby, smoothing my hair and telling me everything will be ok.

"What happened?" He gently probed.

"She was in the wardrobe," I told him, tears slipping down my cheeks once more. "She looks like she's asleep."

"And you're sure she's not?" He asked.

"I've kind of been expecting this," I told him. "She's quite old."

"Where is she now?" He asked.

"I couldn't move her." I looked at him, eyes wide.

"Then I guess I'll have to do it."

I led Ben to the wardrobe and pointed out Maisy's body.

Carefully he lifted her and placed her gently in the box. "What do you want to do?" he asked gently.

"I'm not sure," I replied. "If I had a garden I would bury her, but I don't."

"We could take her to the woods," He suggested.

"Is that even allowed?"

"It's returning her to nature." He reasoned.

The sky was pitch black by the time we set off in Ben's Golf.

We barely spoke on the short drive to the park. Ben carried the box as we headed to the wooded area in the middle of the park. In the absence of a spade, we had settled for the windscreen scrapers that Ben kept in his glovebox.

Carefully we scraped away the earth to create a hole big enough for Maisy.

"Do you think that's deep enough?" Ben asked quietly.

I nodded. I wasn't sure, but I didn't have the stomach to continue digging.

Ben carefully lifted Maisy and placed her in the hole. He stroked her head lightly and whispered "Good night." Before starting to cover her. I imagined my mother's burial. I imagined what that would have been like all those years ago, I wondered who had attended and what had been said. I had never been to a funeral. I felt guilty for missing my mother's.

I shivered as I sat back in the car. Ben turned the heating on and wrapped his jacket around my shoulders.

"Let's get you home." He said, taking my hand reassuringly in his.

"My Mum got me that cat," I told him on the way home.

He looked at me in surprise that I had spoken about Helen.

"It was for my eighteenth birthday." I continued. "I think she had forgotten about it in honesty. She arrived home late one night with this tiny box wrapped in a ribbon. The box was bouncing around. I thought it was a frog or something."

Ben laughed at the thought of being gifted a frog, but I wouldn't have put it past Helen.

"I was so cautious about opening the box. I just didn't know what to expect." I remembered the way my heart had pounded in my chest in anticipation of what might have been in the tiny package. "I untied the ribbon and lifted the lid and this huge pair of eyes were just staring at me. I couldn't believe it. She was so pretty. I stroked her head and she just started to purr and rolled onto her back. She was gorgeous."

Ben didn't respond. He just allowed me to muse out loud. I remembered how thrilled I had been with the gift and the gratitude I had felt. Later I had found out that one of the idiots in the pub had a litter of kittens that his daughters' cat had given birth to. He gave one to Helen in exchange for who knows what and drowned the rest in the sea. It broke my heart when I found out what had happened to Maisy's siblings. I wished I could have saved them all. "What would we have done with five kittens Hope?" Helen tried to reason. "Jesus, that one is enough of a little shit."

I never mentioned the subject again to Helen. I simply tried to keep Maisy out of her way in case she changed her mind and decided to drown Maisy too.

"Will you come in for a drink?" I asked Ben when we returned to my apartment.

"I'm driving." He shrugged.

"You could sleep on the sofa," I suggested. "I could do with a drinking buddy."

"If you're sure." He replied.

An hour later we were sat in my living room. I was gripping my third bottle of Bud, Ben was still on his second.

"What was the worst birthday present anyone ever got you?" I asked Ben.

"The worst?" He shrugged. "I don't know, like maybe socks from my Nan or whatever,"

"Socks?" I laughed. "You can do better than that."

"I guess." He thought for a moment. "I remember my uncle once bought me a National Trust membership."

"That's not a bad gift." I protested.

"It is when you're six." He protested.

I laughed at the thought of a six-year-old Ben wandering around dozens of stately homes.

"So that's it? Your worst-ever gifts were socks and National Trust membership?"

He looked thoughtful for a moment and then laughed a little.

"Actually no." He replied. "I had this great uncle. His name was Erbert. To be honest, I'm not even sure we were actually related, but he and his wife used to buy us gifts at Christmas and for Birthdays. They didn't have any kids and I think they liked to treat us."

"Fair enough." I nodded at the idea, thinking of Jo-Jo.

"His wife Edna died when I was about nine." He said. "We carried on going around there from time to time, but it seemed quite strained and I think he started to suffer from dementia."

"That's sad."

He nodded. "Yeah, it was sad. You know you see this man going from being quite a strong character. A little eccentric but, you know, a good guy basically."

"So, what was the gift?" I asked.

"There were a few." He smiled a little. "So, first of all, he bought me a bottle of whiskey."

I laughed in shock. "How old were you?"

"About twelve." He replied laughing. "My Mum was so polite when I opened it, but kind of said 'I'll look after that for you.' Then all the way home she was ranting away. She kept saying 'who buys whiskey for a twelve-year-old?'" He laughed to himself again. "Her and my Dad polished it. One morning I came downstairs to two empty tumblers and an empty whiskey bottle. My Mum still can't touch whiskey, even now."

I laughed again. "Sounds like a fun gift."

"That was just the start." He protested. "The next year he bought me a stuffed owl."

"An owl?" I shrieked.

"Apparently he had this mate who was a taxidermist and he got it off him."

"What did you do with it?"

"It's still in the loft at my mum's, I think. Daniel and I used to go hanging out in the loft whenever we could. Once they put the owl up there that was it though. There was no way we were going up there with that."

"I'm not surprised," I said.

"The following year was that icing on the cake." He continued. "I was fourteen. A bit cocky and a bit of a know it all."

I rolled my eyes at the thought of fourteen-year-old Ben. I could imagine him wandering the corridors at school as though he owned the place.

"So we rolled up at Erbert's house with the usual box of biscuits and a Christmas cake. He was quite scruffy. He had grown a beard and there were all crumbs in it. His clothes were stained." He looked thoughtful for a moment. "I was frightened of him at the time, though I tried not to show it. He wasn't taking care of himself. He handed me this gift. It was a wooden box. Highly polished with ornate fittings. I think it was pretty old. It was heavy. I had just got into snooker and wondered if it was a snooker set, like a boxed snooker queue and balls. So, I opened this box, dead excited and it was a fucking gun."

"A gun?" I repeated astounded.

"A shotgun." He nodded. "My mum went ape shit there and then. Said 'how dare you give my son a gun?' There was a huge row, Erbert said at least his gifts were original, not the same old shit that he got every year."

I laughed.

"We never saw him after that," Ben said quietly. "Last I heard he was in a care home."

"That seems a shame," I said.

"I think he was happier that way." He laughed a little. "I think the gifts were just a way of trying to get rid of us."

I laughed at the thought of a cantankerous old man who was fed up of the well-wishers so did his best to stop them from visiting.

"What about you?" Ben asked.

I thought of all the presents that Helen had given me over the years. The plastic sandcastle windmill she had picked up on from the gift shop on the way home from the pub, the barely-there thong she had bought me for my seventeenth birthday, the regifted box of chocolates that Jo-Jo had bought her one Christmas. But there was one gift that stood out amongst the rest.

"A pebble." I laughed in a bittersweet way.

"A pebble?" He laughed uncomfortably. "Who got you that?"

"Helen of course." I laughed softly.

"Why a pebble?" Ben looked confused.

"She thought it was nice." I shrugged.

~

I cast my mind back to my fifteenth birthday. By this time I had already set my heart on being an architect. I had researched which GCSE's and A-Levels I would need to get into a good university. I had borrowed several books on architecture from the local library. I would study buildings wherever I went, trying to identify the design era and architectural style. I practised technical drawing as much as possible, but without a proper drawing board, I found it difficult to make my drawings as precise as I wanted to.

One Saturday afternoon, a week or two before my birthday, Helen and I had been in the local art shop picking up supplies. I saw the drawing board straight away. A large A1 board set on adjustable legs. There were drawers and pen holders and an array of instruments. It was perfect.

"That would be perfect for my drawings," I told Helen, trying to draw her attention towards the drawing board.

Helen continued to rummage through the paints. "Hmmm." She responded absentmindedly.

"It's my birthday soon." I smiled.

"Mmmm, so you keep saying," Helen said.

"I'd love that drawing board." I knew that hinting just wouldn't cut it. I had to be direct.

My birthday fell on a school day. I got up early and got ready for school. My mother was still in bed when I left the house. There was no sign of a birthday card or gift, but this didn't surprise me. Nobody at school mentioned my birthday. I was glad to get away with 'birthday digs'. All-day at school I anticipated getting home to find the drawing board I so desperately wanted. I had started to dream up the house I would create.

I almost ran home that afternoon. I heard pop music playing loudly on the stereo before I even opened the front door. The scent of fresh polish was hanging in the air. The house felt clean and inviting for the first time in months. I hung my bag on the hook in the hall and made my way into the kitchen. In the centre of the kitchen table was a small box wrapped in pretty pink paper.

"Happy Birthday." Helen greeted me, strolling in from the sunroom. I was relieved to see that she seemed sober and in a good mood. She wore dungarees with a crop top underneath. She looked pretty and carefree. The sight of her made me smile.

"Thank you." I smiled. It was obvious that the gift wasn't a drawing board, but Helen's demeanour was enough to make up for the disappointment.

"Open your present." She smiled.

I reached for the gift excitedly. The box was quite heavy considering the size. I tore off the wrapping paper, wondering what might be inside. I opened the box. The flash of soft blue wings terrified me. I set the box down on the table and cautiously peered in. Inside the box was a smooth, round pebble. The pebble had been painted. The background was filled with pretty colourful flowers. In the centre of the pebble was a butterfly with majestic blue wings, outstretched as though it was about to take flight. The colour drained from my face, I started to feel sick.

"Don't you like it?" Helen looked forlorn,

"It's err." I looked at her, tears in my eyes.

"I thought it would be personal, something you can keep. I've started a new range of painted pebbles. They've been doing really well in the art shop in St Ives."

"I...I...It's a butterfly." I stammered quietly.

"I've got quite a wide range, the coastal paintings seem to do better." She seemed to be talking to herself now. "I like the butterflies, but that one wasn't quite right. I thought the shape of the wings was a bit off."

"But you know I don't like butterflies," I spoke quietly, almost under my breath. I fought to hold back tears. "You know what happened." How could she not understand what this meant to me? I froze as I could feel the tension in the room.

"You're so fucking ungrateful." Helen hissed. "It took me all day to paint that."

"I'm not trying to be ungrateful." I backtracked. "I think it's pretty it's just..." I trailed off, afraid of making matters worse.

"Forget it." She threw her arms into the air as she stormed towards the door.

~

Ben and I sat up all night, chatting and drinking beer. I told him a little about Helen, I concealed much more. I told him that she had died, but I didn't tell him how.

Ben listened. He hugged me and we cried together. Eventually, we fell asleep in each other's arms.

I was disappointed when I awoke alone on the sofa. A blanket laid carefully over me. I sat up slowly, the dull ache in my head slowing my movements. My mouth felt dry.

"You're awake." Ben greeted me cheerfully.

"Hmm."

He kissed me lightly on the cheek.

"I'm going to let you get some rest," he brushed my hand with his, "I'll call you later."

With that, he was gone. I was filled with the deepest love for this man who had helped me in my hour of need, who had spent the night just holding me because he could sense that was what I needed. After everything I had put him through, I felt undeserving of his friendship.

30

I slept restlessly. Once more my sleep punctuated with bizarre dreams. As I tried to hold on to the images that my mind had formed, they pulled away and lay in tatters. Mischievous fairies called me to play. I was being lifted high above the cliff top, hundreds of tiny hands holding on to my blue summer dress. I made out a figure on the clifftop below. Soft blond curls and full red lips. Ben looked up at me from his precarious spot and smiled his broad smile.

"Hope." His voice was that of a child. "Hope, let's always play together."

"I'd like that." My reply was a whisper on the breeze.

"I miss you." Again, his voice was childlike.

"I miss you too." As I spoke it was as though my words were stolen from me and carried away by the fairies.

"I have to go now." As he spoke, he started to tilt over the edge of the cliff. I saw his body tumbling through the air like a rag doll. Frantically I fought with the fairies in a desperate bid to free myself from their clutches.

"Leave me alone!" I screamed at the tiny creatures.

"You can't save her." The voice had no form, it floated into my ears. "You have to let go of what has gone, you can't bring her back."

I awoke with a start. My head was spinning, my heart was pounding, my mind was a confused haze. I felt a familiar feeling rising inside me. I made it to the bathroom just in time as I threw up. As I sat on the floor of the bathroom by the toilet I began to cry. I was terrified of the thoughts in my mind. Terrified of the dreams that wouldn't leave me. Yet what frightened me more was not knowing what it all meant.

The tiny demon voice rang in my ears, 'You can't save her.' yet it had been Ben who was falling in my dream. What did it mean? Can't save who? Helen maybe? I had tried to save her all of my childhood until she couldn't be saved. Suddenly a thought occurred to me, maybe it was my baby that I couldn't save. Maybe even my mind was telling me that it was time to move on.

Sat on the bathroom floor a thought occurred to me, fleetingly I allowed it to whisper in my mind. 'When was your last period?'

I thought for a moment. I hadn't had a period, not as such. I had the miscarriage, but that was weeks ago. I knew that it might take a while for my body to get back to normal, but maybe? I pushed the thought away, terrified of the implications.

My mind drifted to the day I had discovered I was pregnant when the idea of pregnancy was full of hope and awe. I knew that no matter what, pregnancy would never hold such untainted joy again.

~

It was Saturday morning. Ben and I had started our day lazily. We had laid in bed watching morning TV. I had awoken early from a dream in which Ben and I were making love. As I drifted from my dream-like state, I felt my lips burn with the need to be kissed. I reached for Ben, my lips brushing against his arm. He smiled sleepily. I smiled back as I drew myself on top of him, my lips finding his in the darkness.

"Easy tiger." He laughed as my hand found his erection. "Keen this morning, aren't we?"

"Maybe." I giggled slightly, pulling my top over my head to expose my naked breasts. He gasped before taking hold of them gently with his hands. My breasts felt full and tender. I tried not to flinch at his touch.

"That's ok isn't it?" I whispered as I pushed myself on to him.

"Mmmmm." He sighed as our bodies started to move together.

Afterwards, I lay in his arms. A feeling of contentment emptied my mind of all thoughts. The moments after we made love were always my most peaceful. The horrors that taunted my mind were nowhere to be found. I was able to enjoy the feeling of his arms around me. I could feel his love. I wished that these moments, the feeling of peace and tranquillity could continue until the end of time.

"Would you like a coffee?" I felt a stab of disappointment as he started to rise, although the offer of coffee was rather tempting.

"Yes please." I murmured dreamily.

As he headed downstairs a thought occurred to me. It was Saturday. It should be my period. Well, actually Thursday should have been my period. I picked up my phone to check the calendar, there clear as day was a red dot next to Thursday, indicating that my period was due.

How had I not realised?

My heart started to race with nervous excitement. I jumped up and headed for the shower room, dragging out my stash of cheap internet pregnancy tests. Over the past few years, I had become a pro at testing, I wasn't going to waste ten pounds a time testing my pee when I could buy them for thirty pence each.

I dipped the test into the pot. As I watched the window of the test becoming wet and the pink dye washing over it, I waited with anticipation. I put the test down, a watched pot never boils, but I immediately picked it back up. Examining the results area, desperate to see that line.

As a line started to appear my heart started to pound in my chest. 'It's just the dye, it will go soon.' I told myself. 'It's an evaporation line.' Was my next form of denial.

By the time two minutes had passed the test line was the same deep pink as the control. There was no denying it. It was plain to see, I was pregnant.

I did three more tests before I slipped back out of the en suite, my hands behind my back and a wide grin on my face.

"What's going on?" asked Ben, his brow furrowed in confusion.

"It's pink," I announced.

"What's pink?"

"This!" I squealed as I held up a test.

"Pink?" he asked. "As in pregnant?"

I nodded, barely able to believe it. Ben and I had been trying for a baby since our wedding night almost four years previous. Neither of us seemed to actually think it was going to happen. I had gone from tracking my temperature and drinking herbal tea to just getting on with life and hoping that it would happen sooner or later. Then out of the blue, or maybe out of the pink, here we were with a positive test.

"Are you sure?" Ben asked with caution.

"Take a look!" I showed him the test.

"Wow." He sat on the bed, a smile playing at his lips. "I'm going to be a Dad."

"You're going to be a great Dad," I told him as I kissed his lips.

~

31

In the morning light, my mother's house looked beautiful. The gravel path leading up to the front porch crunched as I drove over it. Stone steps led up to a covered veranda where a swing seat awaited visitors. The pillar box red front door stood out like a beacon against the sandstone brickwork. Pretty leaded windows looked out onto the clifftop like all-seeing eyes.

Nervously I approached the front door. My hand shook as I tried to slide the key into the lock.

Expectantly I swung the door open, almost disappointed by the mundane appearance of the hall. On the left, there were three doors, Helen's bedroom and my old bedroom and the bathroom.

On the right-hand side of the hallway, there were two more doors. The barely used living room was at the front of the house. The door to the large kitchen-diner stood slightly ajar. I could see the familiar kitchen units and dining table through the gap.

I made my way into the kitchen. The kitchen was eerily familiar but strangely sparse.

As I opened the French doors into the sunroom I was hit by the incredible heat. My mother's favourite room in the house was always the one I liked the least. Too hot in the summer and too cold in the winter there never seemed a practical time to use the room. I sat down before my legs giving way. The orange floral pattern on the cushions of the wicker chairs had faded almost to white. Helen's easel and paints were gone. The room looked sad and lonely without her brightly coloured canvases.

I felt sick as I looked down at the stone tiled floor. The image of thick red blood spread out in a pool was etched into my mind. The grout was darker, almost rust coloured in places. Whoever had cleaned up after my mother's parting farewell had done a sterling job, but there were still traces of the past that were visible to those who knew where to look. I shook my head in anger, disbelief, maybe regret.

My mind drifted back to the day I had got my A-Level results.

~

Helen had kept me awake most of the night. There had been loud music, singing and then crying. I had been up and down trying to talk to her.

"Just put away the vodka and go to bed." She gave me an indignant look.

"Why should I do what you say?" She sounded like a naughty child questioning authority. "You know I'm the parent, right?"

"You'd hardly think so the way you behave at times."

I don't know why I was disappointed. It wasn't as though her behaviour was any different than it had always been, but it was getting worse. She was losing control. I could see it and so could she. We didn't talk about the real problem, but it was there and we both knew it.

I had thought about staying put. I had thought about going to a more local university. Mike and Jo-Jo had promised to help. They would keep an eye on Helen, make sure she didn't do anything stupid. Experience had taught me that nobody could stop Helen from doing stupid things.

A sense of unease filled me as I sat eating cornflakes the next morning. I vowed to clean the kitchen upon my return, but right now I had other battles to face. I had told Helen that I had been made a conditional offer at Edinburgh University. I had told everyone that. It was my first choice and as long as I got the results that was where I was headed. Except it wasn't.

"Hey." Claire from my art class greeted me as I walked into the canteen. I smiled at her puzzled that she even noticed me. "This is exciting isn't it?"

I nodded in confusion.

Several tables were set out around the canteen. Each table laden with boxes labelled alphabetically. Students were milling around grasping opened letters. Some were smiling, laughing and cheering with elation, others sat in corners, sobbing as though the world was about to end. As I spotted the box marked "T" I wondered which category I would fall in to.

"I'd better face the music," I told Claire with a nervous laugh.

Miss Brightwell stood guard over the box. As I approached she flashed me one of her cute smiles and a wink.

"Hope." She said warmly. "I'll bet you're excited."

I smiled back politely as she handed me the envelope. I stared intently at the plain brown envelope, as though I could determine its contents just by looking at the outside. I turned the envelope over in my hands. My name was printed in plain bold lettering.

The enormity of the contents hit me. For me, that envelope contained far more than my A-Level results. It represented the sum of my life as a student so far. It had taken lunchtimes in the library, evenings working late, pure hard work and dedication when others played the fool. It represented so much more too. For me, this envelope had the potential to change the whole course of my life. To kick start my path onto a different future. A future that I would never have imagined for myself if it hadn't been for Mike and Jo-Jo and teachers like Miss Brightwell. I closed my eyes and wished. I wished for the results to be good enough for me to at least make it into one of the Universities that had made me an offer.

"Just open it." Miss Brightwell encouraged with a smile.

I braced myself for bad news as I carefully lifted the flap of the envelope. I scanned the paper as I slid it into view. My mouth dropped open as I saw 'Mathematics – A', then 'Art – A'. My heart was racing. 'Design – A', I was elated. 'Physics – B' my heart plummeted.

"Only a B in Physics." The dismay in my voice was palpable.

"Don't you dare!" Miss Brightwell scolded. Stunned I met her gaze. "You have some of the best results in the school! The exam board have taken copies of your art and design work to be used as examples for other students."

"Oh!" Was all I could manage.

"What did you need to get into your first choice Uni?" My mind was blank for a moment.

"Err, three B's." As I replied Miss Brightwell raised her eyebrows.

"So, what are you worried about?" I shrugged.

"It's not that I'm worried, just a bit....." I trailed off as I searched for the word, 'disappointed, frightened?'

"It'll be all right Hope." Miss Brightwell spoke quietly, compassionately. "This is your opportunity to shine, to show people just what you are capable of."

Walking home I felt like Charlie grasping the Golden Ticket. I felt nervous anticipation in my hands, but more than that I felt free. I was uncertain how the future would map out, but that was fine. Mike's voice rang in my ears as I approached the house. 'Aim for the stars, and you might just reach the moon.'

When I arrived home the house was in the same chaotic mess that I had left it. At first, I had wondered if Helen was still in bed. My heart sank when I saw the open vodka bottle on the dining room table. This was an early start, even by her standards.

I rolled my eyes and set down the precious envelope containing my results before I started to clear the mess in the kitchen. There was no sign of Helen, I guessed she was in her bedroom or the bathroom. Helen came shuffling out, of her bedroom. Dark rings around her eyes.

"You're back." She croaked as she shuffled into the kitchen and sat down at the table. I nodded, waiting for her to ask where I had been. She sat unspeaking for what felt like hours. The silence only broken by the sound of the water sloshing in the bowl as I washed the array of dirty dishes.

'Just ask me how I did!' My mind screamed at her through the deafening silence. Every tick of the clock deepened the wound that the silence was inflicting on my heart.

With the dishes washed I turned to face her, my empty face a question mark. 'Why are you like this?' I wanted to ask her. 'Why can't I have a normal mother?' I so desperately wanted her to ask me how I had done. To embrace me and congratulate me and to tell me she was proud. Instead, she sat in a grubby dressing gown, sipping vodka as though it was water.

Defiantly she stared straight back. Her expression made it clear that she would never be happy for me. Angrily I turned and marched toward the front door, leaving the envelope on the table. I grabbed my bag containing my sketchbook and pencils. I needed to forget everything.

I made my way down to the beach. I climbed over the rocks and made my way down to my favourite tiny secluded spot, away from the holidaymakers I sat propped up against the rock and started to sketch the amazing view.

Hours passed before I decided to head back to the house. The tide was starting to wash into my little hidey-hole when I eventually decided to face the music. As I climbed the steps back up to the house I could see a small cloud of smoke. Panic rose in my throat. Had Helen set the house on fire? Adrenalin flooded my body, I ran. My feet beat heavily against the stone as I took the steps two at a time, dodging dawdlers making their careful ascent. 'No, no, no!' My brain shouted the word. As I reached the top of the stone steps I sighed with relief as it became clear that the fire was in the garden. Still, I ran as quickly as my legs would carry me. I opened the front door with one swift push. I ran through the hall, my bare feet slapping on the cold, hard tiles, through the kitchen and into the sunroom. I froze momentarily as I stared out at the sight in front of me in complete disbelief.

The old kettle barbecue stood in the middle of the unkempt garden, orange flames lapping at the sides and dancing high into the air. Helen had the wildest look in her eyes as she danced around tossing papers onto the flames. As she caught sight of me she smiled a broad smile and tossed a brown envelope onto the fire.

Hastily I pushed open the French doors and ran out into the garden. I grappled with the tap and the hose then ran over to the demented scene. I watched as water cascaded over the fire, at first doing little to tame the flames, but eventually snuffing out the treacherous blaze.

Helen was laughing like a crazed witch. The sight of her terrified me. I didn't know what to do, what to say.

It was Helen who spoke first. Her demonic voice cut through the air.

"See?" She screeched. "You're going nowhere now!"

"You didn't?" Pure disbelief took hold of me. Surely not even Helen could do something like this? I studied the brown envelope burned and now drenched. My results.

"It's better this way." Helen protested. "You can't see it now, but you'll thank me one day." I stared at her aghast.

"Thank you?" I screamed. "You're fucking deranged!" My head was spinning, my throat was tight with the tears that I was desperately holding back I needed to stay strong. I couldn't let this woman destroy me.

"What is going on in your head?" As I stood there staring at the woman who had given me life, I felt a strange detachment. She was barely an adult, let alone a mother. That was when I realised. I had outgrown her.

I was tired now of the game that we played, where she would be needy and I would take care of her. I found her cries for help pitiful. I was damned if the rest of my life was going to be controlled in this way. As I turned my back I could hear her starting to sob. Normally that would draw me back, but not today.

32

Tears filled my eyes as I thought of what had passed. “It was my fault,” I spoke the words out loud for the first time. There was nobody to hear them, but they were out in the ether, waiting for the fairies to grasp them from my lips and make them real. Maybe that was what had driven me away all those years ago? The partially formed thought that Helen would never have done what she did had it not been for me. If I had stayed at home and painted with her as she asked then we could have made enough money to pay the meagre bills. My mother owned the house outright so there was no mortgage to pay, besides she spent more on vodka than she ever had on food.

I stood up, angry and confused. The heat in the sunroom was making me dizzy. I knew nothing of my mother. I didn’t know who her family were, what had gone on in her past to cause all of the chaos in her life. I sat racking my brain trying to decide the best place.

My mother’s bedroom was unchanged. Teak wardrobes lined one wall. Her wooden framed bed sat up against the other wall. In the window sat an old dressing table with a tri-folding mirror. I smiled fondly as a thought popped into my mind, a distant memory of a much younger me sat at the dressing table looking into the mirror as my mother brushed my blonde hair. She looked pretty, slim and happy as she made eye contact via the mirror.

“You’re so beautiful Hope.” Her voice was like velvet. “I love you so much, my baby.”

"I'm not a baby." I wrinkled my nose.

"You'll always be my baby, even when you're old and grey."

I pushed the memory aside. What good were happy memories when there were so many more that made me want to scream?

On top of the dressing table sat my mother's jewellery box. Nervously I flipped the latch and opened the lid. The top layer contained a jumble of tangled gold chains. There were studs and sleepers in an undignified mess. Everything in there reminded me of her. Images of her flashed through my mind, half-smiles and glances. Each item brought back a slightly different image, like looking through fragments of torn-up photographs.

The top layer of the jewellery box had ribbon tabs at either side. I took hold of the tabs and lifted it out. Underneath was bare apart from a long, blue velvet box. It looked virtually untouched. I took the box out and prised open the lid. Inside sat a dainty gold watch held in place with elastic. A piece of paper was wedged into the lid. Carefully I pushed the paper out. The paper had faded and yellowed over time. The edges were worn and tattered. As I unfolded the note I was struck by certain familiarity.

My Dearest Helen,

We're in this together, every step of the way.

I love you more than you will even know.

Your knight in shining armour xx

My heart was racing. The watch looked old. I wondered just how old it was. I grabbed the watch and the note the lettering looked strangely familiar. I needed advice.

I parked my car at the St Ives pay and display. I paid for two hours parking, grabbed my handbag and headed off.

I found the old Jewellery shop exactly where I remembered, tucked away in one of the back streets where few people ventured. Gold and silver twinkled on the windows. A bell above the door chimed as I entered the shop. Dust mites hung in the air. The owner sat on a stool behind a long glass counter. A magnifying headband framed his bald head.

He smiled awkwardly, as though someone had once told him that it was important to smile, but he could never quite understand why.

"How can I help you?" His voice was smooth and deep, hardly befitting his frail body.

Nervously I grasped the blue box in my bag and slipped it across the counter to the jeweller.

"I wondered if you could give me some information about this?" I ventured.

He took the box, I could sense his muted excitement. He first examined the box, looking at this part and that. He then opened the box, took out the watch and started to examine it in detail. He pulled down the headband over his eye to allow a close-up view.

He squinted and muttered as he examined the item before finally looking up to meet my eye.

"How much do you want for it?" He asked, straight to the point.

"I'm not certain I want to sell it." I lied. I had no intention of selling the watch. It wasn't mine to sell.

He pursed his lips and furrowed his brow slightly.

"How much would you offer me for it?" I asked to try to win him over.

He shrugged. "Would you take five hundred?" I knew straight away he was trying it on.

"How old is it?" I asked.

"Is it a family heirloom?" He answered my question with another question, I got the feeling that he was growing suspicious. In his line of work, he would no doubt have experience of dealing with all kinds of people trying to pass on stolen goods.

"It's my mother's," I muttered.

He turned the watch over in his hands

"It's an Oyster." He muttered.

"I thought it was a Rolex." As I spoke I wanted to take back the words. The expression on his face told me that I had made a faux pas.

"A Rolex Oyster." He told me with raised eyebrows. I smiled back awkwardly. "It's late seventies, maybe seventy-seven or seventy-eight." My heart skipped a beat. "It has hardly ever been worn from what I can see. Seems a pity not to use such a beautiful watch."

I nodded in agreement.

"The box has quite a lot of wear at the sides," he spoke almost absentmindedly, "as though it's been opened and closed repeatedly. That'll knock a little off the value."

"Thank-you." I held out my hand, my polite smile told him that I would not sell.

"Eight hundred?" He ventured.

"Thank you, but no." My hand was poised to take back the watch.

"Hmm," as he continued to turn the watch over in his hands I was growing impatient. "I know a guy who deals in Rolex watches, he might be able to give you a better price."

"Do you have a card?" I asked in a bid to end the transaction.

Reluctantly he handed me the watch, plucking a business card out from under the desk.

"Thank you." I smiled again politely, tucking the case back into my bag.

33

My mind raced as I scuttled to my car. It didn't take much effort to work out the dates. I was born in nineteen seventy-eight. The watch was from around nineteen seventy-seven or seventy-eight. I was well aware that Helen wasn't one for long term relationships, but had it always been that way? My chest heaved as I gasped for breath. I reached my car and grabbed at the handle, thank god for keyless entry. I collapsed into the seat of my car.

~

I remembered the day that I first asked the question. The autumn leaves had littered the pavement. As we walked to school I shuffled and kicked, watching the swirl of colours as they fluttered around my feet. The sound of the leaves crunching sent shivers down my spine. I slowed my steps as I neared the school.

"Come on Hope." My mother grumbled, pulling on my hand.

"I don't feel good." I lied as I resisted the tugging on my wrist.

Normally I liked school. I liked Mrs Brentford. She was kind and she never shouted at me. She told me I was a good girl and she let me clean the blackboard, even when Amy wanted to do it. Mrs Brentford would ask for a volunteer to clean the blackboard and Amy would put her hand right up in the air, waving it and shouting "Miss, Miss, pick me." But Mrs Brentford picked me more than Amy, even though I didn't shout, even though I only raised my hand a little bit, just enough for Mrs Bretford to see. Amy didn't like it when Mrs Brentford chose me. I stopped putting my hand up when Mrs Brentford asked for people to help in class, 'let Amy do it' I thought. Mrs Brentford stopped asking for volunteers. She just chose people to do the jobs. She would say "Today I'm going to choose helpers who are polite." or "Today my helpers will be quiet children." I liked Mrs Brentford, but I didn't like Amy.

"Don't be silly." Helen tugged again on my wrist. "Let's get going, you're going to be late and then that old battle-axe will have an excuse to make a big deal again."

I tried to stop the tears. There was a lump in my throat that felt like it was choking me. If I concentrated, I could make myself feel ill and then it wouldn't be a lie.

"She's nice," I spoke defiantly.

"Who is?" Helen had stopped and crouched in front of me so she could meet my eye.

"Mrs Brentford." I pouted. "She's not a battle axe." Hot tears rolled down my cheeks.

"Hope we don't have time for this." Helen was trying to be nice, but I could hear in her voice that she was angry. "If Mrs Brentford is nice why don't you want to go to school?"

"Amy isn't nice." There it was out. I'd said the words.

"You have other friends." Helen was trying hard to be nice now.

"I don't have friends." I told her, "I don't mind that, but Amy is mean." My childish mind tried to find the words to make her understand.

"Why is Amy mean?" Helen asked.

"I don't know." I shrugged. I wondered if I should say the words. "She said her mum says she isn't allowed to play with me." I looked down at the leaves crumpled around my feet.

"Why isn't Amy allowed to play with you?" I could tell that she was getting really angry now, but I didn't feel afraid like I sometimes did.

"Jo-Jo says I'm not supposed to use those words." I protested.

"Well, I am your mother, not Jo-Jo, although you wouldn't think so sometimes." She breathed deeply and rolled her eyes. "Just tell me what Amy said."

"She said I'm a bastard," I whispered to my feet. "She said that everyone has a Daddy. She laughed at me when I told her that the fairies had given me to you."

"Yeah," Helen sighed deeply, "Perhaps we should keep that one to ourselves."

I looked up at Helen. I searched for the truth in her big brown eyes.

"Where is my Daddy?" Quickly she stood up swiping at the tears that were forming in her eyes.

"We have to get going, Hope." She took hold of my hand again, avoiding meeting my gaze. "I'll talk to Mrs Brentford about Amy."

~

I sat in the car for what seemed like an age. I barely noticed the quizzical glances from by-passers. I took my phone from my bag and turned it on. I ignored the myriad of notifications and opened Google.

I typed "Rolex Oyster" into the search bar. Within seconds an image of my mother's watch appeared on the screen. My heart raced as I clicked on the image. I scrolled through the blurb from the jewellery company selling the watch. They described the watch as "Rare" and "sought after". The year of manufacture was 1977, the year before I was born. As I saw the price my mouth hung open in shock. Seven thousand four hundred pounds.

"Robbing bastard." I cursed out loud in disbelief.

I took the handwritten note from my bag. It was faded around the edges, as though it had been read over and over. I studied the lettering intently.

It looked familiar, the A's and the E's had a particular slant that made me think of Mike, but then other letters looked different. I had once wondered if Mike was my Dad. He had been so kind to me over the years. He had encouraged me to go to university, pushing aside the obstacles that Helen had placed in my way. Was this the proof I was looking for?

I pressed the start button on the dashboard and put the car into gear. I needed to talk to Mike, but first I needed to do more digging.

34

On my way back to the house raindrops had started to patter on the windscreen. By the time I reached my destination, the rain was pounding on the ground, drenching everything in sight. I jumped out of the car, crouching over to avoid the rain. I felt the cool water splashing through my thin T-Shirt. I tucked my bag under my arm and closed the car door and ran wildly looking for shelter under the veranda. Once protected from the rain I looked out towards the sea. The heavy droplets were spattering on everything in sight. The sea was the darkest of blues. Ferocious waves fought with each other for dominance. The grey sky was angry.

I sat down on the swing on the veranda and looked out to the dark sea. The tumultuous weather matched my mood.

~

I remembered one of my earliest complete memories. Helen and I sat on the swing one the veranda in a storm much like this. Helen was agitated and nervous but trying hard to hide it.

"Where have you been Mummy?" I asked, looking into her deep brown eyes.

"I had to go away for a while, but I'm back now." Her eyes looked sad and empty.

"Jo-Jo says you were sick," I whispered.

"Hmm." I didn't know what that meant so I just put my hand on hers.

"I missed you, Mummy." She lifted me up and sat me on her knee. She wrapped her arms around me and pressed her face into my hair.

"I missed you too Hope, more than you will ever know." Her shoulders started to gently shake as she quietly sobbed.

"Don't go away again Mummy."

"I'll always be here for you Hope." There was such sadness in Helen's voice. "It's just you and me now kiddo, us against the word."

~

Shuddering at the memory I pulled my cardigan around my shoulders.

'Us against the world.' she had told me. If only. Throughout my life, it had felt that Helen had been against everyone and everything. She had been fighting her own demons and had been too self-absorbed to notice anything in my life.

I had sworn to myself that I would be nothing like her, I wasn't sure that I had kept my promise to myself.

In my mother's bedroom, I went to the dresser. Carefully I placed the watch back into the jewellery box.

The dresser had two drawers, one on either side of the stool that I would sit on while Helen brushed my hair. I pulled open the drawer on the left. I smiled to myself as I discovered the jumble of make-up. Half used foundation bottles and lipsticks. I picked out my mother's favourite pink lipstick and applied it to my lips. I stared at my reflection in the mirror, was my likeness to her in my imagination? I was fairer than her. I felt as though I looked younger than she did, the years of drinking hadn't been kind to her face. My nose was the same, my high cheekbones just like hers. I realised I had forgotten her face. Not entirely, but it was no longer etched on my mind as it had been. I needed to be reminded.

I dragged the dressing table stool over to the wardrobe and reached up to where I knew my mother had kept photographs.

I pulled the box from the shelf and dropped it down onto the bed. In the box was a jumble of images. Each photograph evoked a new memory. I paused at an image of me stood proudly next to a sandcastle. A huge grin on my face. That day Helen had been sober. She woke me up early. A look of excitement in her eye.

~

"We're going to the beach." She announced enthusiastically.

"Ok?" I struggled to focus on her smiling face.

"Come on," she threw back the duvet from my bed, "I've made bacon and egg for breakfast."

"You cooked?"

"Hey, cheeky!" She seemed quite indignant. "Don't try to make out I never cook."

I decided not to argue, but I really couldn't remember the last time Helen had cooked anything.

As I sat eating breakfast I looked around the kitchen. It was spotless. The windows had been cleaned, the floor mopped. Even the oven had a certain sparkle. As I ate Helen stood at the sink washing the pans that she had used to make breakfast.

"How's school?" The question came out of nowhere.

I shrugged. "OK." I thought for a while. "It's a bit weird having so many different teachers, but I like the fact that I'm not always with the same people." The transition to high school had been smoother than I had expected. There were more people to ignore me, but provided I kept my head down most of them did just that. My daily mantra was 'don't make them see you'. I had been at the new school for three weeks, this was the first time Helen had mentioned it other than to complain about the cost of the uniform.

"But you're happy aren't you Hope?" I had no idea how to answer that question. I wasn't even sure if I knew what it meant to be happy. I got by. Each day I put one foot in front of the other and I did what I could to stay out of trouble. Avoiding trouble featured heavily in my life.

I shrugged again, this time looking at her, my head tilted to one side questioningly. "Is anyone ever happy?" The words surprised me as they erupted from my mouth. "You're not happy, Jo-Jo isn't really happy, even her nephew Mike who owns the cafe seems sad most of the time."

Helen stood against the sink, quietly cleaning the dishes. When she had finished she came and sat facing me. Her brown eyes searching mine.

"Nobody can be happy all of the time Hope." She spoke softly. "But Mike is happy. Jo-Jo is happy too."

I looked her in the eye. "You're not happy."

"I'm working on it." She replied. "Let's make today happy and we'll go from there."

And that was what we did. We played in the sea, we played volleyball and then we worked together to build a huge sandcastle. Helen took a full reel of photographs that day, as though she was desperately trying to make up for the times when she had been too drunk or too sad to even look at me, let alone photograph me. As we walked back from the beach she took my hand in hers, gently yet affectionately.

"Thank you, Hope."

I laughed. "Thank you for what?"

"It's been a lovely day." She said.

"It has, hasn't it?" I smiled warmly, relishing the affection between us.

~

35

The sound of the doorbell startled me. The rain was still pounding the ground. The sight of Kevin and Amy on the front porch was entirely unexpected.

“Oh, Hello.” I greeted them with surprise.

Amy had gained weight, I wouldn’t have recognised her had Kevin not been with her. Her face looked tired.

“Mike said you were coming over to the house,” Kevin announced. “We thought we’d bring you some supplies.” I tried not to cringe at the bottle of Chardonnay that he held up. Amy held up a bottle of milk and tea bags.

“Oh, thank you.” I forced a smile. “Come on in.”

As I led the way through the hall and into the kitchen I couldn’t shake the memory of the last time Kevin was in this house with me. The bloody paw prints had been erased from the hall floor, but they were forever etched on my mind. I wondered if Kevin remembered that night in the same vivid way that I did.

“Would you two like a glass or would you prefer tea?”

“Oh, just a tea for me at this time,” Amy replied politely. I got the impression that she was here under duress. I wondered if Kevin had told her about the kiss we had shared so many years before.

“Me too,” Kevin replied. As I filled the kettle with water I struggled with the uneasy atmosphere. I couldn’t help but wonder why they had decided to pay me a visit.

"So how does it feel to be back home?" Amy asked awkwardly. I thought about the question for a moment or two. The truth was that this wasn't home. It hadn't been home for such a long time. Stepping through the front door felt like stepping into a dream world. The memories that it evoked were painful in so many ways.

"I'm still staying at the Meadows." I dodged the question.

"Why?" She looked confused.

"I'm not sure I could stay here overnight." I replied honestly. "It's not easy for me to come here."

She nodded, but I wasn't sure she understood.

"Have you been into town?" Kevin asked.

"A couple of times," I replied. "I went down to Catchers and saw Mike." I looked at Amy. "Your Dad looks well."

"Doesn't he?" She replied. "I want to know his secret."

"He had some sense to get out of the fishing lark," Kevin said.

"I didn't know he had worked on the boats." I had always thought of Mike as being the owner of Catchers keep, I had never considered that he had a life before he opened his cafe.

"Yeah," replied Kevin, "he used to have a boat with his brother James, but when James was killed in an accident he decided to give up the life."

Did I imagine Amy giving Kevin the death stare?

"I didn't know Mike had a brother." I pondered.

"It was years ago," Amy said dismissively. "I didn't know him, he died before I was born."

"That's a shame," I replied sadly.

"He doesn't talk about it." It was clear from her tone that she wanted to end this line of discussion.

"I've not seen you since that night at the beach." Amy shocked me by changing from one taboo subject to another. My eyes widened as she spoke. "You know everyone was looking for you?" There was a tone of accusation in her voice. "My dad and Aunt Jocee logged a missing person's file, but because you're not next of kin the police were sparse on the information they would give."

I focussed on the cups as I stirred the tea, avoiding her stare. "I didn't think anyone would look for me." I met her gaze momentarily. "But after everything I needed a fresh start." I placed the cups on a tray and walked over to the table. Smiling sweetly as I placed one before Amy and another in front of Kevin.

"After about six months the Police confirmed that you were safe," Kevin spoke more carefully. "Mike and Jocee were happy to hear that, it was enough."

"It was inconsiderate though." Amy spat the words. "To just up and leave without a word to anyone."

I remained surprisingly calm. "You weren't there Amy. You have no idea what my life was like, you were lucky enough to have a family who took good care of you, you were popular at school, you didn't have to put up with bullies." My heart pounded as I spoke the words, but I didn't let the adrenalin pumping through my body betray me. "You may think it was inconsiderate of me to leave, but I have seen Mike and I have seen Jo-Jo. Neither of them reprimanded me in any way. I'm sorry if I caused some disruption to your family. I assure you that I didn't intend to worry or hurt anyone."

"I'm not being spoken to like this." Amy stood up. "Kevin we're going." I was stunned as Amy marched through the house. Kevin shrugged apologetically and followed.

I sat quietly at the kitchen table sipping my tea. The empty house felt suffocating. I was left with my thoughts and distant memories. I was aware that a missing persons report had been logged shortly after my departure from Port Merdow. I wasn't sure who had logged the report, but I had assumed it was Jo-Jo.

~

It was early spring. Winter had passed and the world was starting to reawaken. The trees around campus were full of fresh buds that spoke of new beginnings. My maths lecture seemed to drag on forever and the interruption from the department head was somewhat welcome. He whispered into the Maths tutors ear.

"Hope Michaels." When the tutor called my new name I almost ignored him. I was yet to own my new name. "Hope?" he spoke again, making eye contact this time.

"Oh uh." I flustered, feeling all eyes upon me.

"Could you go with Dave please?"

"Yeah, of course." Quickly I packed away my books and pens and rushed to the door, almost tripping on the way.

Dave led me to a small room next to the maths class.

"Try to relax Hope," he told me quietly. "PC McGovern is here to make sure you're OK." My eyes widened as he led me into the room. Sat at a table was a police constable in his late thirties. His hair was greying at the temples. His face was kind and gentle.

"Hope?" He asked as I entered the room.

I nodded.

"Take a seat." He smiled. "Can you confirm that your name is Hope Tegan?" he asked as I slipped into the seat opposite him.

"I changed my name." I protested. "By deed poll. I made sure I did it properly."

He nodded, "But you were Hope Tegan?"

"Yes." My voice was barely audible. My heart was racing.

"Your last known address was Treth Chy in Port Merdow?" He struggled as he read the house name from his paperwork.

"Yes."

"You were last seen on Saturday the 15th of August?" He asked.

"Yes." I nodded quietly, a lump forming in my throat as I thought of that day.

"I have had a missing persons request logged." He told me. "Now you're over eighteen so I am not obliged to divulge any information to the person who logged the report, but I do need to check that you are safe and well."

I nodded. "I'm fine," I told him. "Please tell Jo-Jo, sorry Jocee, that I'm fine and that I'm sorry. I didn't have much choice, not after everything. I just needed a fresh start."

He looked at me and nodded.

"I need to ask if you're being held against your will." He told me.

"No, I'm not being held by anyone."

"Do you want me to pass on your address?" He asked.

"Please don't." I pleaded. "I just need a fresh start."

"OK." He nodded. "If you're sure?"

"I'm certain," I told him.

"Well, all that remains is for me to wish you good luck." he shook my hand as he left. I remained seated, barely able to move.

Dave occupied the empty seat that the constable had left.

"Are you OK Hope?" He asked gently.

I nodded, afraid to speak in case the tears started to flow.

"You've been very brave." He told me. "I have a little information about your history, I know that it's not been easy for you, but I can see that you're very determined to succeed."

"Don't tell anyone what you know." I pleaded. "I don't want to be treated differently."

~

36

My mind was still occupied with my thoughts when I wandered back into my mother's room to tidy up the photographs. I'd had enough nostalgia for one day.

As I stood on the stool to put the photographs back I was surprised to see a box labelled "The summer of love." I had a burning desire to see what was inside. The flowery pattern on the outside of the box looked like Helen's handy work.

Carefully I lifted the box down. I lifted the lid to find that the box was filled with dozens of photographs. The colour was washed out on many, but my mother's face was unmistakable. There was a photograph of Helen stood on the beach, pure happiness in her eyes. There was another of her stood next to a deep blue fishing boat. The name the 'The China Doll' was painted on the side. My mother was pointing at the name, an excited grin on her face. Another showed her sat on the clifftop near Treth Chy, her back was to the camera as she looked out to sea.

The bittersweet photographs brought tears to my eyes. She had been happy. Truly happy. The look of pure abandonment in her face couldn't be replicated. Her happiness brought me joy, but it also brought sadness. Was I the reason she drank? Was I the reason she committed suicide?

I threw the photographs back into the box. I was about to replace the lid when a familiar face caught my eye. I pulled the photograph out from the pile. Helen looked pretty and young in the photograph. Her face was filled with joy and love. She was gazing lovingly into a pair of kind eyes.

Mike's arm was draped lovingly around her, his other arm resting on her round pregnant belly. It was him all along. Mike was my Dad. Heart pounding, I tucked the photograph into my pocket.

The rain had kept the tourists away and Catchers Keep was empty. I spotted Mike sat at the blue chesterfield chair that had always been my favourite. He was sat sipping coffee and sorting out paperwork. A broad smile started to spread across his face as he saw me, but his smile dropped as I neared him, a crazed look in my eyes.

"It was you all along!" I shouted the words at him as I pressed the photograph down in front of him. "All the time I thought my Mum had just got pregnant to some randomer and it wasn't, it was you!"

"Hope, wait." He raised his hands in surrender.

"What about your wife? What about Amy? Do either of them know what was going on behind their backs?" I fought with the tears as anger bubbled within me.

"Hope, sit down." His calm voice only served to infuriate me further.

"You can't talk your way out of this." I stared him straight in the eye.

"Hope, it's not what you think." He stood up, walking towards me with his arms open wide. "That's not me in that photograph."

I sat down, stunned. I remembered the look Amy had given Kevin when he mentioned Mike's brother.

"Hope it's my brother." His voice was soft and gentle. He sat down next to me, grasping my hand. "It's my twin brother James."

Tears glistened in his eyes. He looked pained.

"James?" I repeated quietly. "Was he my Dad?"

Mike nodded. “Helen and James were together,” Mike said. “Your grandparents were unhappy about them being together, they wanted Helen to go to teacher training college, to have a career. They didn’t think James was good enough for your Mum.”

“I’ve never met my grandparents,” I told him.

“When your Mum became pregnant, they cut her off completely. James bought Treth Chy and he and Helen set up home.”

“Kevin said you had a brother,” I spoke quietly. “He said that there was an accident.”

“We had a fishing boat.” There was such sadness in Mike’s eyes. “One day James went out in a bad storm, he never came back.”

“Why did nobody tell me?”

“Helen insisted that you weren’t to know,” Mike said. “She said that if you knew that James had died that you would have a sense of loss throughout your life.”

I laughed at the irony. Helen had tried to protect me from feeling an emptiness in my life but had created a void that she had filled with fairy stories.

“I always had a sense of loss,” I spoke angrily. “I lost my father and I never had a mother.”

“Helen was more of a Mother than you give her credit for.” I was angry at Mike for defending Helen. I was sick of hearing about what a great person she was.

“I’m glad you’re so well informed!” My voice was thick with sarcasm. “I’m glad you understand what it was like waking up every morning and not knowing. Not knowing what state she would be in, who would be there, how she would react.”

I turned to leave, tears springing from my eyes.

“Hope, wait!” Mike called.

"I've found out what I needed to know," I told him. "I wish I'd never come here, this town is filled with nothing but bad memories."

I headed back out into the rain. The cold water drenched my T-shirt. I shivered against the cold as I stormed through the rain.

Tears streamed down my face as I wandered the streets aimlessly.

'Why did you come here?' My mind screamed. 'What did you hope to find?'

A whisper of a voice cut through my thoughts. A tiny blonde-haired girl sat on a picnic blanket sipping tea. She lowered the cup and looked up to meet the gaze of my mind's eye. 'You know the truth, Hope. It's time you stopped pretending.' The voice sent shivers through my spine. I closed my eyes, pushed my hands over my ears.

"No!" I screamed. "Leave me alone!"

37

As the rain soaked my skin I thought of Helen. “You need your raincoats today girls.”

An image of shiny red wellington boots popped into my mind. Splashing and giggling as I jumped in freshly formed puddles.

“I’m going to jump in that really big one there.” An image flashed through my mind of a little smiling face surrounded by a mane of soft blonde curls. A bright red, hooded rain Mack and matching red boots.

“Faith.” The word was a lightning bolt through my brain. I was struck to the core. I started to run, my feet squishing into the mud as I ran towards the clifftop.

I stood looking out over the stormy sea. The salty wind whipping my hair, rain lashing down. I was in turmoil.

I closed my eyes and returned in my mind to the bright summers day when life changed beyond anything that anyone could have imagined.

Brightly coloured butterflies danced all around, the sound of children laughing filled the air. I felt safe and happy and relaxed in that moment, so full of life. Little had I known it, but that moment had been pivotal to so many lives. A metaphorical fork in the road. Had life taken one path then things would have remained the same. I wondered if life would have been different, I would have been different, Helen would have been content. I knew in my heart now that right here on this cliff is where Helen’s journey into hell had begun.

I remembered running through the tall grass. I remembered the feeling of the warm sun and the smell of pollen hanging in the air. The sight of hundreds of brightly coloured butterflies dancing through the air.

I remembered Faith.

I stopped with a deep inhale of breath as the image of my twin appeared in my mind's eye. Soft blond curls bobbing around her little head, she turned to face me, bright pink lips broke into a beaming smile.

Butterflies filled the air. Hundreds drifting through the air. Brightly coloured wings carried them this way and that. I giggled with excitement as I reached for one of the butterflies, my fingers brushed its wings as it flitted away from me. Faith was laughing, running ahead. I ran faster trying to catch up with my stronger sibling. Excitement filled my tiny body as I ran reaching for the butterflies, dancing and skipping. In that moment I was overcome with love for Faith.

My double, my partner in crime as my mother always called us. The bond we had shared was unique and beautiful. We were one, sharing thoughts and feelings, each the knowing others pain.

Faith and I ran through the grass without a care. Reaching for the enchanting creatures who coaxed us further away from Helen. Faith was in front, picking up speed she ran faster and faster, turning to catch my eye, joy gleaming in her blue eyes. I reached for a blue butterfly perched on a flower. I expected it to dart away in time, but it didn't! Victory! I held my hands in the air. "I got one I shouted", searching for Faith to share my prize. "Faith?" I called her name. The most dreadful noise echoed around the cliff tops. It wasn't a scream, it wasn't a cry, it was more guttural, closer to the sound an animal might make when in utter pain.

My muscles contracted with fear. I felt confused and afraid as I was scooped up into the arms of a stranger. Reaching out and shouting "Mummy!", hot tears rolling down my face.

I caught a glimpse of my mother, lay in a heap at the edge of the cliff, screams bursting from her throat. In my hand, the blue butterfly was squashed and lifeless. Hot tears rolled down my cheeks.

~

I opened my eyes and looked down over the cliff edge. I saw the jagged rocks that lay below. Faith had fallen onto those rocks. I imagined my doppelganger lay in a broken heap. "It was my fault." The thought plagued me. "I killed her." I wanted to turn back the clock, roll back all of the years that had passed and change what had happened. I wanted to warn Faith to turn, to stop running, to watch where she was going, but I couldn't change the past. I felt powerless.

We had all been broken by the events of that day, Helen had never recovered from the loss of the daughter she loved so dearly, so much so that she had forgotten that she still had me. She had become so lost in her pain and from that day onwards appeared to hit the self-destruct button until she could take it no longer.

I sat down on the cliff edge and I let go. My body heaved with pain. I cried for Faith, I cried for Helen, I cried for my own unnamed, unborn child. But mostly I cried for myself. For the choices, I had made. The way I had been hiding my whole life, pushing people away in order to protect myself. I had always thought I was hiding from my mother, from the feelings her memory evoked. I now realised I was hiding from the day we lost Faith.

"Hope!" Mike stood a few feet away.

"Why did nobody tell me?" I jumped to my feet, as I screamed the words, anger and confusion bubbling through my body.

"Helen wanted you to have a normal life?"

"What the fuck?" I knew I must have looked like a madwoman, hair flying in the wind, rain lashing my face and body. "What the fuck was normal about my life with Helen?"

"She really tried, but she had severe depression." He sounded utterly sympathetic.

"So she drank herself into oblivion?"

“Unless you have suffered the pain of losing a child you won’t understand.”

I looked at him, mouth open wide. “I have just lost a child! I had a miscarriage! Because I never got to meet my child you think it’s so much easier? You think it’s better to have lost a child that you never got to hold? That you never had the opportunity to protect?”

“I know what you’re going through is difficult Hope, but it’s not the same.” Anger bubbled up inside me.

“How would you know what’s the same?” The words spewed from my lips in a hate-fuelled eruption. “You with your perfect life and your perfect fucking daughter who could never put a foot wrong! I was just eighteen when my mother killed herself! I never knew my father and I had to make my own way in the world. I have fought for every single thing I have and I fought for that child and I loved it more than life itself before it was ripped from me.”

“Hope, come away from the edge.” There was tension in Mike’s voice.

“I’m not going to jump for Christ's sake!” I turned my face away from him. “Just because Helen took the easy way out doesn’t mean I’m going to.”

Mike’s hand reached out for mine. “Hope I think you misunderstood.”

“I pulled my hand away angrily. As I did the movement set me off balance, I stumbled backwards, my feet slipping beneath me in the mud. Terror filled me as I felt my body falling backwards, and then I was yanked forwards. Mike’s strong hand grasping my T-Shirt and pulling me forwards. He pulled me towards him, wrapping his arms around my tiny body.

“Helen didn’t kill herself.” He whispered in my ear.

38

Darkness had fallen over Treth Chy. The storm had lifted and there was a stillness in the air.

I had washed and changed into a pair of old jeans. I was sat on the sofa facing Mike, my hair still wet.

"What did you mean when you said that Helen didn't kill herself?" I asked nervously. "Did someone else do it? Helen had plenty of enemies."

"No." He said quietly. "Hope you need to promise me you're going to stay calm though. You're still in shock."

"I'll try." My eyes pleaded with him. "I just want to know the truth."

"You know how hard Helen found things. How she suffered so much with depression?" I nodded. "She blamed herself so much after Faith died. She was riddled with guilt. She was terrified that something would happen to you too." I thought of all the warnings she had given me about keeping away from the cliff edges. How I was never allowed to go anywhere without her or Jo-Jo.

"I get that." I agreed.

"I guess she just started to drink away the pain, I think she thought she could handle it." It sounded strange to hear Mike being so sympathetic towards my mother. "When you got those results and you were headed off to University, she was afraid. She drank herself into oblivion. I think cutting her wrists was a cry for help. She had expected you home much sooner and I think she wanted you to find her and realise how much she needed you."

"That's not much better." I told him, "Either way she died at her own hands."

"No," Mike argued. "When you found her, she had lost consciousness. She had lost a huge amount of blood. Her vital signs were slipping away but they managed to stabilise her in the ambulance. They gave her a blood transfusion."

I struggled to comprehend his words.

"She's alive?" I barely dared to ask the question. Over twenty years of believing that my mother was dead. Over twenty years of guilt for leaving her. Over twenty years of wishing I could turn back the clock.

Mike nodded. "She suffered huge trauma from blood loss. She's in a care home near St Ives."

"You didn't say." Tears filled my eyes once more.

"I was waiting for the right moment," Mike said. "The blood loss caused a brain injury, she isn't the Helen you remember."

"Is she alone?" I asked, suddenly the thought of my mother alone and confused bothered me.

"I see her every week." He replied. "She has friends there. She paints. She isn't in so much pain."

I nodded. I felt numb. I tried to process my thoughts.

"Do you want to see her?" asked Mike.

I shook my head. "Maybe in time, but not right now."

I hugged Mike and thanked him before I climbed into the driver's seat of my car. I promised to return, but I was unsure if I would keep the promise.

I set the Sat Nav to 'Home'. I knew there was so much to tell Ben. So much that I had kept hidden, even from myself.

~

I smiled to myself as I thought of Ben. It came as a surprise when the phone rang about a week after I lost Maisy. Ben's face showed up on the screen. Excitedly I pressed the green button to answer the call.

"Hello?" I spoke nervously into the phone.

"Hey there." He sounded drunk.

"Ben?" I knew it was.

"Hope." I could hear music and voices in the background. "How are you?" he slurred his words.

"I'm OK," I replied in confusion.

"Whatcha up to?"

"Reading a book," I told him.

"Is it a good book?"

"Yeah," I replied. "The Shining, but I'm not sure I should read it when I'm in the flat on my own, I won't be able to walk past fire hoses or anything." I rolled my eyes at the absurdity of my comment, I wasn't sure if he had read The Shining and I had no fire hoses in my flat. Would he get the reference?

"Ha, you need someone to look after you."

"I've managed so far." I kicked myself for not flirting back. I was terrible at flirting. "But I need to thank you for last weekend. You were amazing."

"I'm glad you've finally realised how amazing I am." I could imagine a cocky smirk on his face.

"It had to happen one day I guess." I laughed.

"I'm out with some people from work."

'No kidding' I thought.

"Are you having a good time?" I didn't know what else to ask, but it was one of those moments where I was expected to speak.

"Something is missing Hope." His voice was empty. "It's just not the same without you here."

He had put into words exactly how I had felt for such a long time. I would see a joke and think to myself 'Ben would find that funny.' I missed him.

"Well let's meet up for a night out next weekend," I suggested.

"Let's go one better." I could hear something in his voice, anticipation, a nervous excitement. "Come to Barcelona."

"What?" I laughed nervously. "Barcelona? Why? What? When?"

"Come on." He purred. "You told me how much you loved it when you went with Uni, but that was years ago. We could visit all of the Gaudi buildings and take in the atmosphere."

"Why do you suddenly want to go to Barcelona?"

"Because I'm sat here drinking flat overpriced beer in a crap pub with a load of people who I couldn't give a toss about and all I can think about is you. I'm thinking to myself 'what would Hope like to be doing now?' I think that given a choice you would be in Barcelona with me rather than alone reading Stephen king and giving yourself nightmares."

I laughed. "Maybe."

"And I know," he continued, "that I'd rather be anywhere with you than here with these idiots."

I laughed again. "Do me a favour, Ben." I smirked as I spoke. "If you remember this conversation in the morning, and if you still want to go to Barcelona with me then call me when you're sober."

I lay in bed dreaming of walking through the pretty streets of Barcelona. I was stood gazing in amazement at Casa Batllo. The door to the building was closed. Ben was stood hammering against the door, desperately shouting let me in. "It must be closed," I told him. "We can come back tomorrow."

The hammering continued, the voice drifting into my mind. Sleep drifted away, yet the banging continued. As consciousness took over, I realised the knocking was not in my dream, it was outside. I grabbed my dressing gown and headed downstairs. As I opened the door I was greeted by a mop of dishevelled curly blonde hair and a lopsided grin.

"Let's go to Barcelona." Ben stood grinning at me.

39

Six months passed before I plucked up the courage to return to Cornwall. This time Ben and I took the journey together.

"Should I come in with you?" Ben cradled my hand in a supportive gesture as we sat in the car park of the care home.

"Give me a few minutes alone with her," I asked.

I had phoned ahead and spoken to the staff of the care home to ask if I could visit. They had been thrilled to hear from me and encouraged me to make the journey.

My heart was beating more quickly and my throat became dry as I approached the doors to the reception. I paused nervously before stabbing at the bell for the telecom system.

"Can I help you?"

"It's Hope O'Donnel," I spoke into the telecom. "I'm here to see Helen Tegan."

"Come on through." The voice chirped.

In the reception, I was greeted by a pretty girl with a welcoming smile.

"Hi Hope," she extended her hand. "it's so lovely to meet you. I'm Millie. I'm one of Helen's main carers."

"Nice to meet you." I shook her hand. "I'm a bit err…"

"This must be difficult for you, it's been a long time." Her eyes were full of sincerity.

"I thought she was…." Tears started to sting at my eyes as I spoke.

"I understand." She spoke softly. "Why don't we go and see her, she's in the garden."

Obediently I followed Millie through the home. She spoke as we walked and I drank in the sights. The corridors were adorned with artwork. I recognised some of Helen's pieces. The home seemed quiet and calm. I wondered if it was always this way.

"Helen is one of our longest-serving residents," Millie told me. "We have talked to her about independent living, but I think she likes the company of the other residents and the staff."

"She has a house in Port Merdow, it's where I grew up," I told her.

"Yes, she has told us about the house," Millie said.

We walked out into the garden. It was a pretty garden lined with trees and flowers. My heart skipped a beat when I saw Helen sat on a bench in the corner of the garden. Her hair had lost its lustre and her face had been touched by time, yet she looked healthier than I ever remembered. She was carrying a little more weight too. Her eyes didn't carry the same pain as before. She had an easel and a set of watercolours and seemed to be looking intently into space and daubing on her canvas.

Nervously I approached and sat down on the bench next to her.

"Do you mind if I sit here?" I asked cautiously.

"No, that's fine." She smiled. "Do you know what's for lunch?"

"Err, I'm not sure." I was a little perplexed by the question.

"It's probably cottage pie, it normally is on a Tuesday." She told me. "I prefer lasagne myself, but we normally have that on Thursdays."

"Oh." Was all I could manage. The whole situation seemed surreal. Here I was sat opposite my mother after more than twenty years of thinking she was dead and all she could do was talk about the menu.

"I've been out here all morning." She patted the bench. "It's nice being out here rather than sat in my room."

I smiled and nodded.

"I've got my room nice though." She continued. "Not like some of them in here, some of them just sit rocking all day, I like to keep busy. I do my paintings and I keep my room nice. I have a nice bed, it's got a lovely bedspread with embroidered butterflies. I ordered it online, I have a tablet and I can just go online and order whatever I need. I ordered some nice white trousers last week. They look really good on me."

"Do you like it here?" I tried to change the subject. I had not known what to expect. I knew my mother had a brain injury. The woman in front of me looked like Helen, her voice sounded like Helen, but it wasn't really her. All of my life I had hoped to see a better version of my mother. I knew it had been futile to expect that now, but I had hoped for more.

"It's ok." She replied. "That Millie is a bit of a pain. She doesn't like me talking to people too much."

I smiled and raised my eyebrows as she shuffled to the end of the bench to get closer to me.

"If she sees me talking to you she might come and tell me to leave you alone, she's a bit of a busy body."

"It will be fine," I told her. "I want to talk to you."

"So how come you're in here?" she asked.

"I'm just visiting," I told her. She raised her eyebrows and nodded as if to say 'that's what they all say.'

"When is the baby due?"

I rested my hand proudly on my round, pregnant belly and smiled.

"About three weeks." I replied, "We're having twins."

Suddenly that struck a chord. She opened her mouth momentarily, lost in thought.

“I had twins.” She spoke almost to herself. Such sadness in her voice. “They were the most beautiful girls you have ever seen. Such pretty blonde curls and bright blue eyes. They were so bright and clever too.” She smiled fondly, but there was a dark shadow in her eyes as she spoke.

“What were their names?” I felt a little foolish asking the question I knew the answer to, but I wanted to encourage her to talk about Faith and I didn’t know how else to do it.

“Hope and Faith.” She replied dreamily. “But I lost Faith, there was an accident when she was three.” Helen’s eyes filled with tears as she spoke into the distance.

“I’m sorry to hear that.”

“It was a long time ago, but…...” She shook her head, unable to find the words to express the loss. “Then, well I let my other girl down.”

“In what way?” I felt like a fraud for asking, for pushing her to talk about this difficult subject.

“I just couldn’t look at her the same. The girls were identical, you could barely tell them apart. Once Faith had gone I’d catch a glimpse of Hope and for a moment I thought it was Faith. It broke my heart.”

The blood drained from my face. “I can imagine,” I spoke quietly.

“I lied to Hope.” She spoke once more. “I made her think that Faith had not been real. I just couldn’t stand her asking for her all of the time.” Helen shook her head. “It was a dreadful thing to do.”

“I’m sure she forgives you.”

Helen looked at me. For the first time since I had arrived, she really looked at me. For a moment I thought I saw a fleeting recognition in her eyes.

“I truly hope so.” She whispered. “I’m tired now.”

I nodded. “Nice to meet you.” I smiled.

“Maybe you’ll come again some day.” She inquired cautiously.

“I’d like that.” I patted her gently on the shoulder as I turned and left.

I placed my hand gently on my large belly. I felt my twins wiggle beneath my touch and smiled. I couldn’t wait to meet my girls. I would never forget the baby I lost, but I wouldn’t allow that loss to destroy my chances of being a good mum. My babies needed me to be strong for them.

Ben was waiting in reception.

“How did it go?” He asked, concern in his voice.

“It was strange.” I replied. “but I think it’s been a help.”

“Yeah?”

“Let’s go home.” I took his hand in mine and kissed his cheek gently.

My mind wandered as we took the long journey home. I slipped back in time.

Epilogue

In the stillness of the night screams erupted from my throat. In my mind butterflies were everywhere, their soft wings taunting me in the darkness. “Faith,” I called out weakly and first. “Faith!” I shouted, then sobbed. “I want my Faith!”

Mummy appeared dressed in a white nightdress. Her feet bare, her eyes red and swollen. Her body was bent and exhausted. Her whole being exuded sorrow.

“Hope.” Her voice was soft as her bare feet padded across the floor to my bed. She sat down beside me, her head in her hands in an expression of despair.

“I need Faith.” My voice was sad and desperate, searching for comfort.

Helen shook her head in despair. “I can’t do this.” She spoke into the darkness. “I told Jo-Jo I haven’t got it in me to carry on.”

“I’m frightened Mummy,” I told her, desperate for her to take me in her arms and comfort me. Desperate for her to show me we were safe and that everything would be ok.

“You need to stop this Hope.” Tears filled her eyes, but she demanded them not to fall.

“But I need her Mummy.” I pleaded with her. “She’s a part of me.”

“You’re too old for an imaginary friend.” She spoke bluntly. “That’s why I took her bed away. It wasn’t right to keep pretending.” I glanced towards the space where Faith's bed belonged. The emptiness magnified by the missing chunk of my heart.

“But I wasn’t pretending.” I protested.

“It’s nice to pretend when you’re little.” Helen continued. “But you’re growing up now, you’re a big girl. It’s time to let her go.”

I was confused and frightened. I didn't like seeing my mummy so sad. I didn't want to upset her.

"When you have the dreams about Faith you need to say 'Go away, I know you're not real.' If you say that, if you really mean it then the dreams will stop and then everything will be OK."

"But." I started to protest, fear growing inside me.

"Please no more arguments Hope, I'm so tired." I could see in her eyes how true that was. She lightly placed her hand on my forehead, I wanted her to hug me, but I still found the gesture a comfort. "go back to sleep now Hope."

She patted me gently on the head.

"Everything will seem better in the morning."

Nicole Thorne

The China Doll

BOOK 2: SECRETS AND LIES SERIES

A Prequel to Chasing Butterflies
The China Doll

Helen is a fragile young woman who dreams of becoming an artist.

James is a traditional fisherman who longs to break free of his parent's expectations.

When James and Helen meet, the chemistry is undeniable.

When an unwelcome visitor arrives from Helen's past her new found happiness is thrown into jeopardy.

Is their love enough to save them from the dangerous paths they are starting to follow?

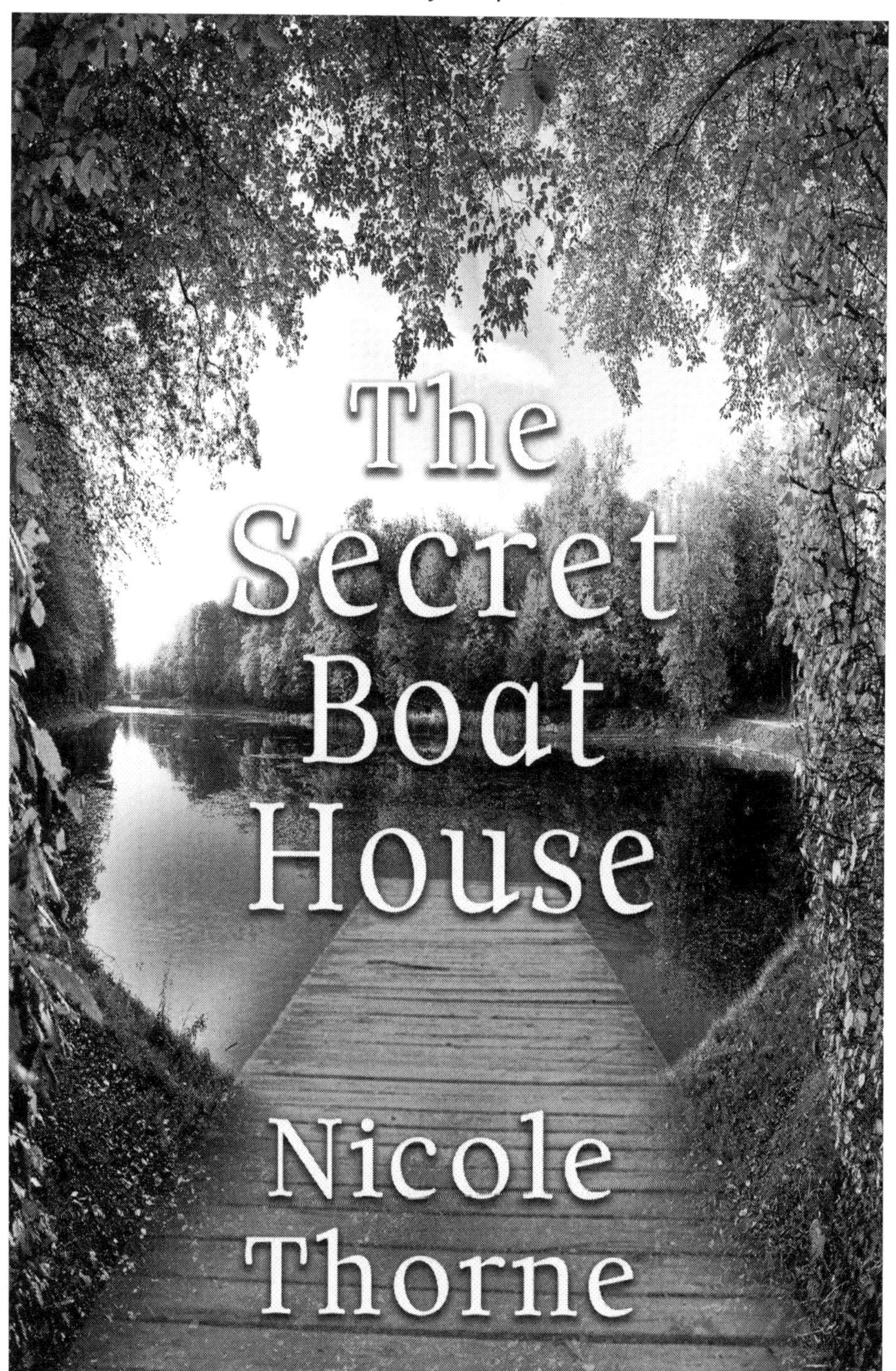
The
Secret
Boat
House
Nicole
Thorne

Coming Soon...

The Secret Boat House

Will and Beth's tender first love blossoms in the Boat House, lost in the middle of the forest.

Years later when orphan Jack and Will meet, they strike up an unlikely friendship that helps them both to heal their wounded souls.

Yet the secrets from the past threaten to destroy everything.

Nicole Thorne

The Restless Tide

BOOK 3: SECRETS AND LIES SERIES

Available to Pre-Order

The Restless Tide

Part 3 of the Secrets and Lies trilogy.

Hope and her Mother, Helen are rebuilding their relationship as Hope helps Helen to strive for independence.

Helen is taken on an emotional journey into her past as a grim discovery.

About the Author

Nicole lives with her family in the North West of England

Nicole is a former teacher with a passion for books and reading.

Her books feature flawed characters that readers can relate to.

Follow Nic on social media

Facebook: NicoleThorneAuthor

Twitter: @NicThorneAuthor

Instagram: @nicolethorneauthor

https://nicolethorneauthor.wixsite.com/website

Printed in Great Britain
by Amazon

60556805R00137